Treacherous Turnabout

In that instant Amos and two of the ranchhands came through the door. They were all carrying rifles and they had them pointed at us.

"Well, Mister Smart Aleck Robber, the laugh's on you. We'll just take that money." And he cocked the goddamn hammer of the Winchester he was holding.

"Now hand it over. And maybe we won't bury you behind the barn."

Other books by Giles Tippette

Western Fiction

THE BANK ROBBER
THE SUNSHINE KILLERS
AUSTIN DAVIS
WILSON'S GOLD
WILSON'S LUCK
WILSON'S CHOICE
WILSON'S REVENGE

Fiction

THE TROJAN COW
THE SURVIVALIST
THE MERCENARIES

Nonfiction

THE BRAVE MEN
SATURDAY'S CHILDREN

WILSON'S WOMAN

Giles Tippette

A DELL/ELEANOR FRIEDE BOOK

AN ELEANOR FRIEDE BOOK

Published by
Dell Publishing Co., Inc.
1 Dag Hammarskjold Plaza
New York, New York 10017

ISBN: 0-440-19636-1

Printed in the United States of America

First printing—January 1982

To Betsyanne
The first and last woman
I'll ever love

WILSON'S WOMAN

Chapter One

~~~~~~

Hell, I'd jumped back and forth across the border from Mexico to Texas and Texas to Mexico so damn often that sometimes I near forgot which law was chasing me the hardest.

This time me and my two partners had just arrived in Galveston, Texas, having taken passage on a steamer out of Tampico, whence we'd arrived after a desperate flight from the Mexican authorities who was after us for robbing a bank in Sabinas Hidalgo.

First place we headed for in that port city was a bar. I wanted time to think and to decide what we should do. We were way off our range, which was normally down around the border, and I was feeling a little uncertain as to what to do next. One thing, we had plenty of money, about eight thousand dollars a man, counting what we'd got off robbing that payroll up in the Panhandle and then what we'd taken off that Mexican bank.

We come walking down that wharf, coming off that ship, lugging our saddles and what little gear we had in our saddlebags. Galveston was a pretty big city. I'd heard someone on the boat say it would run nearly twenty thousand. Well, that was pretty big as far as I was concerned. The biggest city I'd ever been in was El Paso, when we'd robbed that poker game, which had been rated at near thirty thousand. But, somehow, Galveston seemed bigger. I guess because it was kind of more close in and confined.

We come into town feeling just the slightest touch out of place. Here we were wearing them bigbrimmed Texas hats and boots and carrying them low-slung guns on our hips and ever'body else was walking around either in good broadcloth suits or else they looked like some of them sailors we'd had on that boat we'd taken out of Tampico.

But then I was used to feeling out of place, or at least outside of where most folks were. I'd been on the owl hoot trail since I was seventeen, and I was coming toward the age of thirty-five in that year of 1892. I reckon in terms that most people think in I hadn't done all that well with my life. But I'd finally come to the place where I'd had to say, "All right, I'm Wilson Young. I'm an outlaw. And I been in the robbing and killing business too long to get respectable. So now, by God, I'll just try and make a good job of it."

Now I wasn't no murderer. Except for that gunman who'd killed my partner up in the Panhandle, I'd never killed a man where I had a selection and could get out of it. Of course, to my shame, a number of men had died either by my hand or as a result of something I'd done. I had the reputation for it and I was feared by any number of men, but it wasn't something I was proud of. To tell you the truth I had just sort of wandered into the outlaw business right after the Civil War when the carpetbaggers and scalawags had robbed my poor daddy of his ranch holdings down around Corpus Christi, Texas. I'd drifted into the business for want of another way to make a living and then had spent a number of years trying to gain enough money to reform and become respectable.

But I never had no luck getting out of the profession. It seemed as if one thing or another had come along to defeat me so, in just the last little while, I'd just sort of surrendered to what was evidently my destiny and decided to go in the direction my stick seemed to be floating.

Don't think, though, that I still didn't yearn for all that other men had: a good home with a good wife and a family. Don't think I liked living hand to mouth as a man in my line of work has to do. Don't think I liked all them cheap hotels and greasy spoon eating houses. Don't think I like constantly looking over my shoulder and feeling that every man's hand was against me. Don't think I wouldn't have traded it all in a minute for a quiet little settled life and a woman who loved me and I could be true to.

But I knew that it wasn't going to be, so I figured just to make the best of it.

One thing I'd been lucky in had been partners. I guess a man's got to take his blessings where he can, and partners, good partners, had been mine. I cannot say they'd had the best of luck with me, though, for I'd managed to lose a good number through the years. But that, I'd resolved, was a thing of the past. Les Richter had been the partner I'd regretted losing the most. I had not been with him, when he was killed, but any man that's had a friend like Les Richter will never get over wishing he was still around.

I guess that's part of what had made me take on Dennis Wilcey, for when we'd joined up some several years back, it had been his likeness to Les that had made me take to him from the first, even though he'd had no experience in the outlaw business. Oh, they didn't exactly look alike. But Wilcey, like Les, was tall and spare and kind of loose jointed. He was near as tall as me at six feet one inch, but he couldn't come up to my 190 pounds. I reckoned their real likeness came from that little sardonic grin both of them would give me when they thought I was taking things a little too seriously. Wilcey was awful bad about hoorahing me, though he could act the old maid himself at times.

But he was a good man. The best, I reckon, that I'd known since Les. He'd been a rancher up in the Panhandle whose wife had run off with another man, taking their children with her, and the blow had sent him to drink and lassitude to the effect that he lost his ranch and near everything else he had. He'd saved himself by becoming a gambler, and I'd met him in Sanderson, Texas, when I was on the run from some bounty hunters and he'd been of good service in saving my life. It had been me that had brought him in to outlawry, and even though he said he liked the life, there were times I had grave doubts that I'd done him any favor. Like I say, he was a good man. He was steady in a stormy situation and he was a cool head, but he was not particularly good with a gun and he worried a little too much for his own good. But the main thing was I didn't feel he was of a hard enough stripe to handle the life.

But he hadn't let me down yet, and I was content that he should go on being my partner.

Chulo, on the other hand, my other partner, was quite a different matter. For whatever Wilcey lacked in hardness and meanness, Chulo more than made up for. He was easily the meanest-looking man I'd ever seen. He was very dark, so dark that we called him the black Mexican or Nigger. He'd lost an eye in a train robbery that he and I had pulled, and the eye patch he wore did nothing to make him look any kinder. Then he had a knife scar on his cheek and that, and his big hawk nose made him look like someone you'd go plumb out of your way to avoid. I'd very often used Chulo to scare someone into submission or

to threaten that if they didn't do something I'd turn
Chulo loose on them.

It seemed to work every time.

But then it wasn't bluff, for Chulo would do damn
near everything I told him to. He was a simple,
uncomplicated man who thought I'd hung the moon
and who was perfectly content to take my orders.
Sometimes, when there was a disagreement between
Wilcey and I and Dennis would appeal to Chulo for
support, he'd just shrug and flash them white teeth in
his black face and say, "But Weelson *es el jefe*. The
boss."

He was also a hell of a man in any kind of fight.

So we three come walking into town, leaving the
harbor where all the ships were and entering what
looked to be the downtown section. It looked a little
strange to me. We'd been used to adobe and Mexican
tile, and all these buildings were made of clapboard
with shingle roofs. Some of them were even up on
stilts. The reason being, as I'd been given to know,
that sometimes the water got up so high it'd get in
your house if you hadn't raised it up.

Which seemed like a damn silly way to me to live.

Wilcey said, "Where we headed, Will?"

"Well," I said, "first we're going to find us a hotel
to stay in and get shut of this heavy gear we're lugging around. Then we'll find us a good saloon and
have a few drinks and just kind of generally cool out.
After that I reckon we'll see what this here town has
to offer in the way of a little good times. I figure we
owe that to ourselves."

We found a hotel just a little off the courthouse
square and got us a couple of rooms. Me and Wilcey
taken one together and the black Mexican bunked in
by himself. That hotel was three stories tall and we
were on the top floor. Looking out the window, we
could see the bay and some of the ships in the harbor.

A few were steam powered like the one we'd taken out of Mexico, but most were still tall-masted sailing ships.

After we were settled in, we changed shirts and then went downstairs and got the desk clerk to put our money in the hotel safe, just leaving out enough for what we figured we'd spend. I've put money in banks before and probably will again, but it ain't a practice I like to make a habit out of. I guess the business I'm in gives a man a certain mistrust of banks.

Then we all wandered out on the street to see what was going on. It was near the noon hour and things were a little crowded, but there wasn't no shortage of saloons and we found one in good order and settled down at a table and ordered a round of good brandy. When it come we all said luck, then knocked the brandy straight back as befits the toast.

I said, "Aaah. That's damn good brandy."

Wilcey said, "Will, how safe you figure we are here?"

I shook my head. "I dunno. I figure it's about six of one and a half dozen of the other. On the one hand it ain't likely they'll be looking for us on this range. But, at the same time, we don't exactly fit in the crowd around here, not dressed as we are and looking like what we are."

"You give any thought to what we're gonna do?"

I shook my head again. "No, not really. We got plenty of money for the time being, and I think we ought to just rest up for a while. I'm anxious to go see what that Houston looks like. They tell me that place is so big it's about a half a day's ride to get across. We ought to be able to do some business in such a place. I'd reckon there was a power of money there. But for right now let's just lay around here and see what happens. I understand, because of all these sailors that's in and out, that they got some of the fin-

est whorehouses in Texas." When I said the part
about the whorehouses I happened to glance at
Chulo and see the glint come into his one good eye.
I nudged Wilcey. "Look at that damn *Meskin* gettin'
all heated up. That sonofabitch would fuck a wildcat
if he could get somebody to hold it."

Chulo laughed. *"Seguero. Como no."* Of course,
why not.

Oh, he was some tough *Meskin*.

But Wilcey said, "You're talking about doing some
business in Houston. You reckon we ought to do that?
I mean, if we ain't all that bad wanted in these parts,
why not leave it so and do our business elsewhere?"

I looked at him. "Wilcey, when you're in the robbing business, you're in the robbing business, and you
do your business everywhere you find yourself."

"Well, I just don't see the point of it."

"Wilcey, don't start acting the old woman again.
You know what this was going to be like when you
got in to it. Don't you understand that we ain't safe
no where, no time, no how? Now let's have another
drink and not worry about business for the while. My
mind, right now, is on finding a woman."

And, truly, I was nearly froze for one.

We had a couple more drinks, inquired from some
men where the local whorehouses were, and then
sauntered out the door and down to a street called
Post Office Street, which was right down near the
wharfs. To be handy to the trade off the ships I figured.

We found a likely-looking place and went in.
There was a big room right after you went in the
door with a lot of girls sitting around and a good
number of those sailors. We took a table, ordered a
round of drinks, and went to looking over the pros-
pects. It was a two-story whorehouse with stairs going
up to the rooms on two sides.

I immediately noticed that this was a different kind

of whorehouse than I'd been used to. It was bigger and nicer, for one thing, but the main difference was that very few of the girls were Mexican, which is what you mostly find in whorehouses down on the border. I also noticed that Chulo looked mighty out of place in the joint. As near as I could figure he was the only Mexican man there. I didn't know what difference that was going to make, but the last thing I wanted was any trouble.

The drinks came and we knocked them back for luck and then kept on sitting there looking over the girls. I don't particularly like to be with whores, but a man in my occupation don't have much choice. He really ain't in the situation to go calling on the parson's daughter with a nosegay in his hand. But I did have to say I'd had more opportunities than most. However, with my luck, I'd managed to misplay them. Mainly because of a little highborn senorita that I'd carried in my head and heart for more years than I cared to remember. And that without the slightest chance of winning her. And, as a consequence, I'd let my chances at several good women slip away from me, women who knew who I was and what I did and were willing to take their risks and try and make me a wife.

Well, I'd always been a damn fool where women were concerned.

About the only smart thing I'd ever done where the fair sex was concerned was finally to get that little highborn senorita out of my heart. I'd done that on the robbery in Sabinas Hidalgo.

And had damn near got my partners killed in the doing. But they were good men and willing to take their risks even when it seemed I'd gone out of my head.

So now I was very much womanless again and feeling it pretty strongly. I'd had some talks with myself in the time I'd had on that boat, and I'd decided I'd just have to sleep in the bed I'd made. And if that meant having nothing but whores, then so be it. I had no one to blame for it but myself.

It was coming late spring and it was a warm night. Even though they had the front door open to the place, it was still hot and smoky and noisy. Occasionally one of them drunk sailors would bump into our table and make an apology in some strange accent. This Galveston was one of the biggest ports in the South, and as a consequence it drew ships from all over the world to pick up cotton and beef and hides and other stuff that people in Texas had to sell. I'd been through the tenth grade in school, and I knew where England and Ireland and France and those other countries were. I'd never seen anybody from there, nor heard them speak, but I figured that's where most of the sailors were from—some of them countries.

Wilcey said: "Well, you made a selection?"

"I kind of like that blonde over yonder," I said, nodding toward where a kind of plump girl with fair hair was sitting. She was wearing a red velvet dress with ruffles around the bottom and a low bodice. She made me think of Hester, the woman I'd tried to bring back from the Panhandle with me. Of course the only reason she should remind me of Hester was that they was both fair haired. For where this woman was plump, Hester had been slim and raw-boned, and Hester would have looked about as right in a red velvet dress as a pig in ribbons.

About that time a sailor went over and sat down on the settee by the woman. Wilcey said, "Well, looks like you've drug your feet too long."

"Naw," I said, "that's going to be a high-priced woman and that sailor ain't got the kind of cash necessary. He's just over there hoping to get a free feel."

Chulo said: "I theenk I go now." He flashed them white teeth in his black face and got up.

I called after him, "Now stay out of trouble, Chico. Understand?"

He looked back at me, grinning again, and then headed for the girl he'd picked out.

I said: "I pity these poor goddamn women in this place. As long as he's got money in his pocket he's going to wear out a few of them."

But I was more than just a little worried about the Nigger. He sure looked off his range. We all did, but him more than any other, and if anybody was to cross him or give him the slightest insult, there'd be trouble and bad trouble at that.

I didn't say nothing about it, though, for Wilcey worries enough without me giving him any help.

I said to him: "You seen one you like yet?"

"Aw," he said, "I ain't in no hurry. You go ahead. I'm just going to sit here and drink awhile."

I stood up. The sailor didn't look like he was making much progress. I figured he was trying to get her down on the price, but she sure didn't look like the kind that was offering a bargain, not as crowded as the place was.

Wilcey said: "Now you stay out of trouble."

"You too," I said. I looked at him. "Keep an eye on Chulo if we get separated."

A drunk sailor bumped into me, but I shoved him out of the way and walked on over to where the lady was sitting on the little upholstered bench. She and the sailor looked up. I said to him: "You buying or just looking?"

He give me a kind of look that made me believe he didn't understand. "Buy or git," I said. I said it in a kind of hard voice and he understoood that all right.

He got up and vamoosed. I looked down at the lady. "Well, darlin'," I said, "I got money. It ain't just talk. What have you got?"

She looked up at me. She said, "Thank God, a Texan. I swear I'm so goddamn tired of all these Frogs and Eyetalians and Limeys I could scream."

I said: "Com'on. I'm going to pick up a good bottle of brandy at the bar and then you and I are going upstairs and go to war."

She got up. "You ain't askin' the price?"

I said, feeling my throat getting thick and that old copper taste coming into my mouth, I said: "You just let me know when my money runs out."

She said: "Honey, I think I'm going to love you."

Which was all right with me, even if I was paying. A man in my trade has got to take love where he can find it. No matter what kind of love it might be.

Well, I stayed with her until about three in the morning. Her name was Marianne and she was twenty-five years old and said she was from Dallas. She'd been in the whore business about five years, but she was the nicest lady I'd been around for a long time. I didn't realize how hungry I was for a woman, and for hours I just tried to bury myself in her soft, white body. I put a lot of my pain and a lot of my hurt and a lot of my fear in her, and she took it all and left me feeling almost near whole again. When it come time to leave I asked her what I owed and she said twenty. I tried to give her fifty dollars, but she wouldn't take it. Which was damn unlikely behavior for a whore. But at the door of her room she put her arms around me and said, "You just come back and see me tomorrow night, cowboy. And come early so I don't have to put up with none of them goddamn sailors."

I walked back to the hotel in a pretty good mood. It might be a pretty good stay in Galveston, what with Marianne and all. I got up to the room and got undressed and got into bed feeling tired but pretty damn good. I was still thinking about Marianne's soft, white body when I dropped off to sleep.

I felt like I'd been asleep about five minutes when I felt myself being shaken awake. I started to react, to flip off the bed and come up with my gun, but then I heard Wilcey's voice saying, "Will! Will! Will, wake up! Wake up!"

I was half sitting up on the bed. He'd lit the gaslight. I was still about half asleep. I said, "What? What?"

"Wake up! We got trouble."

"Shit, Wilcey!" I said. I sat up and swung my legs over the side of the bed. "What time is it? Goddamn!"

"Little after four," he said. "Here."

He stuck a bottle of brandy under my nose and I took it and had a sip. It tasted awful as foul as my mouth was. "Give me some water," I said. While he poured me out some in a glass, I sat there rubbing my face and trying to wake up. He poured a little brandy in the water and I swished some around in my mouth to clear out the gum and then spit in on the floor. Then I had a pretty good drink and some of the cobwebs began to clear. Wilcey was standing in front of me watching and waiting. Finally I looked up. "Well?"

"Chulo killed one of them sailors. Shot him in a whorehouse."

"Oh, shit!" I swore. "Goddamn him! Well, where is he? Is he in jail?"

Wilcey shook his head. "No. I got him out of there. I've got him hid out in a warehouse down by the docks. But I don't reckon he can stay there long."

"Damn!" I said. "Damn, damn, damn. And damn

him. I told him to stay out of trouble. Well, how'd it happen?"

He shrugged. "Aw, Chulo and this sailor got in to a argument over some girl they both wanted and the sailor came at Chulo with a knife. Chulo just outed with his pistol and blew a hole in him."

"Is he dead?"

Wilcey laughed shortly. "I reckon he is. Though we didn't hang around to make sure."

"Did it happen in that place we was first at?" Asking that made me think of Marianne and made me even more regretful about our need to get out of Galveston now.

Wilcey shook his head. "Naw. When you didn't show back up, Chulo wanted to go on down the street and find some different girls. So I strung along with him like you told me. Don't seem like I did much good, though."

I said: "Don't worry about that. At least he ain't in jail."

"Will, what are we going to do?"

I shook my head. "I don't know this second. Let me think." I held my head in my hands and tried to figure what to do.

The hell of it was we didn't have any mounts. We couldn't take our horses on board the steamer so we'd got shut of them in Mexico. We'd planned to buy some the next day, but that wasn't doing us any good of the moment. We could maybe steal three horses, but there ain't no faster way to go to drawing attention than to start stealing a man's horse. You steal a horse it ain't just the law looking for you, it's everyone.

Finally I said: "Hell, let me go and see how he's fixed. See how long he can hide out where he is."

Wilcey said: "Not long, I'm afraid."

"Well, we got to have some time. If he can't stay there we got to figure out a place he can."

I told Wilcey to go on downstairs and wait on me at the next street corner. "Ain't no use in you and me being connected. Somebody's got to stay on the loose. When you see me coming you just go to leading and I'll follow. Stay about fifty yards ahead of me."

He left and I got dressed, strapping on my big 44/40, which is a Colt .40 caliber revolver on a .44 frame. The advantage to that is that a .40 caliber cartridge is going to stop anyone you need to stop, and the heavier frame of the .44 makes for steadier shooting. It, like all my other weapons, is the finest money could buy. As you could well imagine, men in my line of trade have to have the best guns and the best horses. Sometimes that is the only difference between going on and a short end to your career.

The lights were on in the lobby when I got downstairs, but the desk clerk was leaned up against the wall, sleeping standing up. He never even noticed me go by. I got outside and looked up the street and saw Wilcey standing there waiting for me. I walked toward him and he turned and started for the docks.

As late as it was you'd of thought the streets would have been deserted. But, no, they was some diehards still going at it. There was even a pretty good number of saloons still open. And down by the docks they had the place lit up with gaslights and looked like they were loading ships. I tell you this Galveston was a going place.

Which was part of what was worrying me. I didn't know how city law worked. I knew about border lawmen and the law in Mexico and about sheriffs in little Texas towns, but I didn't know anything about this city law. I'd even heard that some of them wore uniforms.

Just how hard would they search for a Mexican

that might have killed an English or Irisher sailor? You never knew. Maybe they wouldn't give a damn, maybe it happened all the time and, so long as you didn't kill one of the townsfolk, they didn't particularly care.

It had been self-defense, of course, but we were hardly in the position to go to the law and plead that cause. They might let Chulo off on shooting the sailor, but they'd hang me and Wilcey and him for about a hundred other deeds.

Ahead Wilcey had stopped in front of the doors of a big warehouse. It was pretty dark so he waited for me and then we slipped through the door, which was about half open.

Inside it was even darker, and we had to stand a moment to let our eyes adjust. When my eyes come around, I could make out stacks and stacks of bales of cotton and barrels of salt beef. No question, they'd be working this warehouse the next morning. Chulo couldn't hide out here very long.

Wilcey said in a low voice, "He's just over here, back in the corner."

We went a little ways and then Wilcey gave a little whistle. There was no answer and he whistled again. Again there was no answer and Wilcey swore softly. "Now where is that damn *Meskin*! I left him right over there behind them bales of cotton in the corner."

Of course we didn't want to slip up on him for fear of being shot in the uncertain light.

But we went ahead, kind of edging around the bales until we got to the clear place in the corner. Down on the floor, his arms folded, his hat over his eyes, was Chulo, snoring slightly.

I looked at Wilcey and said, sourly, "One of these days that *Meskin* is going to worry himself to death."

I went over and gave him a not-too-gentle kick. He

reacted suddenly, reaching for his big pistol, but I stopped his arm with my boot long enough for him to recognize me. He grinned, his white teeth flashing even in the dark of the warehouse. "Hey, Weelson. *Qué pasa, amigo?*"

I squatted down beside him. "You goddamn *Meskin*, what'd you have to kill a man for? After I told you to stay out of trouble."

He furrowed his brow, looking puzzled. "But, Weelson, he had the knife. I shoot hem for the knife."

"Aw, shit!" I said disgustedly. "One of those little baby sailors? You could have taken the knife away from him. Damn you, Nigger!"

His face took on a pained expression. If anyone that looked as mean as he did could look hurt. He said, "Why you fuss me, Weelson? I shoot plenty mens and you don't fuss me."

"Aw, shit!" I said. There wasn't any use trying to explain to Chulo the difference between killing a man in a border brawl and killing one in a big city like Galveston. I said: "Oh, forget it. Right now I got to figure out a place for you to hide until tomorrow evening. Until I can get us some horses and we can make a getaway under cover of night."

He said: "I stay here. *Como no!*"

"*Como* not." I said. "Because there'll be workmen in here in the morning moving this stuff on board ships and I don't think they'll take you for one of them. No, you stay right here while I look around. Wilcey, stay with him lest he go back to sleep."

I walked out in the middle of the warehouse. There was a big door leading out the back and I stepped through that. I was on the docks, just as I'd suspected. The waterfront was only a few feet away. There, tied to dockside, were any number of boats, bobbing in the swell, in size all the way from big two masters down to dories and rowboats.

I stepped to the dock's edge, looking at the boats, wondering if there were some way I could slip Chulo aboard one of them without him being noticed. But even if I could, likely I'd pick one that was sailing with the tide and Chulo would wake up about half-way to France.

Still thinking, I went walking down the dock edge, looking around. There was a little light from the gaslights on down the wharf, but it was still dark enough that when I heard a voice near at hand, I couldn't immediately see who it was.

The voice said, "Here, lad, what's your business here?"

I stopped. "What?"

A man suddenly materialized out of the dark. He was short and stocky and wearing a cap like sailors wear. He was carrying a double-barreled shotgun under his arm.

I said: "What the hell are you?"

He said: "That's what I be askin' you, lad. I be the night watchman for this stretch of dock. Now what be your business?"

From the sound of him he was Irish, but that shotgun didn't have no nationality. He wasn't exactly pointing it at me, but it wouldn't have taken much to raise it.

I said, carefully, "I'm just taking the night air. I'm a cowboy and I never seen the ocean before."

"Oh," he said, looking me over. "Well, it ain't an ocean, lad, it's a bay. Galveston Bay. Now that you've seen you be on about your business and come back when it's light, lad."

I started to turn away and then I had a thought. Hell, after all he was Irish. I swung back to him. "Say," I asked, "would you take a bribe?"

He looked a little surprised. "Come again, mate?"

I said: "I'm talking about money. I got a friend I

need to hide out until dark tonight. If you know of a place down here and could help us fix it up, it'd be worth fifty dollars to me."

You could see it had taken him aback. He stood there, his mouth working. "Fifty you say?"

"Yes." I figured fifty was about what he made a month.

He got edgy. "Why does the lad have to be hid? Has he done something awful?"

I gave him a wink. "Husband trouble. He's been grazing on another man's range." I got up two double eagle gold pieces and began slowly clinking them in my palm.

He looked down, licking his lips nervously. He said: "Just until this night, eh?"

"That's it," I said. "Nothing more. Just so long as he don't get found. See, the husband's brought charges and the law might be looking for him."

"Aaah," he said. "It's a shame how some people get so upset about nothing." He looked around, studying the boats. "Let's walk down this way a bit."

We walked down the dock about twenty yards, and he halted in front of a little single-masted vessel about forty or fifty feet long. Then he looked at me. "Fifty dollars you say?"

"In gold. Cash in hand."

"Then give it to me," he said gruffly. He held out his hand and I put the gold coins in his palm. He said, jerking his head toward the little single master, "The lads off this boat won't be back for three, four days. Your friend could hide there until night, and if the lad stays below, no one will find him."

I said: "Well, we're going to kind of make sure of that. Me and a friend of mine will stand guard turn and turn about here on the dock to make sure nobody wants to go on board." As I said it I kind of loosened my gun in its holster. "And he's got as big a pistol as I do."

He looked at me quickly, and I think it suddenly hit him that he wasn't dealing with no cowboy.

"No need for that," he said, but he said it a little weakly.

I got a match out of my pocket and struck it on my breeches leg and then held it up so that it created some light. "Step closer, friend, and let me get a good look at your face. If anything goes wrong I want to be able to find you."

"Here now," he said, "Here now! No call for such talk. If Sam Johnson says he'll do something and takes a man's money, then by God Sam Johnson will do it."

"Good for you, Sam," I said. "Now you walk clean up to the end of the dock while I bring my friend out. Be best for you if you didn't see him."

I watched as he walked off until he disappeared into the dark. He was grumbling to himself, but I could hear him clinking them gold coins in his hand.

When I was convinced he was good out of sight, I ducked back inside and got Chulo and Wilcey and hurried them out to the dock. At first the Mexican was reluctant about getting into the boat, but I told him if he didn't get in the goddamn boat and damn fast, I was going to throw him in the water. We got him over the side and he stood there, trying to keep his balance against the sway of the boat and only making it worse by the way he was flinging himself around.

I pointed out the little cabin door. "Now get down there. There'll be some bunks or something down there, and you get down there and close the door and stay there. Now move, goddamnit!"

He went through the little cabin door, looking unhappy, and closed it behind him.

I straightened up and lit a cigarillo, feeling relieved.

"He be all right?"

"I think so," I said. I told him what had happened with the night watchman. Then I said: "Now I want you to go on back to the hotel and get you about three or four hours' sleep. I'm going to stand watch here. You come back and relieve me and I'll get a little sleep and then go and buy us some horses."

He said: "I'll take the first watch."

"Naw. Go on. You ain't been to bed at all. But bring me back some coffee and brandy when you come."

He disappeared and I settled up against a handy wall and got ready to wait out the dawn.

Chapter Two

〰〰〰〰〰〰〰〰〰〰〰〰〰〰〰〰〰

It was a long vigil. After about an hour the night commenced to get a little gray as the sun started out from the horizon way over across the water. But even as it got up it didn't get light right off. There were still little low clouds of fog laying over the water and out over the bank. I had smoked I didn't know how many cigarillos and I still had plenty of time to wait before Wilcey would show back up. Lord, I was tired. It wasn't the first time I'd ever been up all night, but it damn sure felt like it.

Finally the sun burned all the fog off, and I stood there, leaned back against the building just waiting for the time to pass. There were workmen now, coming up and down the dockside, and coming out of the warehouses with bales and barrels. They'd give me a glance, but then go on about their business. I wondered how Chulo was doing. Sonofabitch was probably laying down there sleeping like the dead. Him that had caused us the trouble. And here stood I, dead on my feet, a fool to the world, standing there guarding him so nobody could go down and interrupt his nice sleep.

Well, the damn black bastard. He'd get his in the by-and-by.

Once he stuck his head out the cabin door, but I

immediately waved my hand violently at him and he ducked back inside.

Finally Wilcey showed up, rubbing his eyes.

"Anything happen?"

I shook my head. "Naw. You bring me that coffee and brandy?"

"Hell. I forgot it."

"No matter," I said. "I'll get a drink on the way to the hotel, but I don't reckon I'll need much to put me to sleep. I don't know what to tell you to do if somebody tries to get on that boat with Chulo. But try and start as little more trouble as you can. If you can't stop them peaceably, then get him off and make your way back to the hotel."

"I'll handle it," he said.

"I'll be back before noon. You get anything to eat?"

"I grabbed a quick breakfast. You go on and get some sleep."

I left the docks, walking back toward town. The city was up and astir, and, by God, it was still a going place, even in the mornings. On my way I passed the whorehouse that I'd been at the night before. My thoughts turned to Marianne and I thought for a second of going in and seeing her. The door was open and there were even a few drink patrons sitting at the tables, though none of the girls were visible. I paused, but I was too tired and she was more than likely asleep. I went on to my hotel and then to my room, first leaving word at the desk to have someone wake me before noon.

I fell asleep the minute my head hit the pillow. I didn't even bother to take off my clothes or my boots. The next thing I knew someone was pounding on the door. I come boiling out of bed, grabbing my revolver and trying to clear my head enough to remember where I was.

It was only the desk clerk at the door.

"What?" I yelled.

He said, through the door, "It's half past eleven. You wanted to be woke up."

"Yeah. Thanks."

I put my revolver back in its holster, then went over to the washstand and poured me out a basin of water and washed my face, trying to get the sleep cobwebs out of my brain.

After that I had a stiff drink out of the bottle of brandy we had in the room and commenced to feeling better.

I went downstairs and sought out a café, stopping on the way to buy a newspaper to see it there was any news about the killing Chulo had done. In the café I got settled and ordered me up a bunch of grub. I was plenty hungry. When it come the food proved to be a little different. On the border we were used to beef and beans. Here they give me steak and creamed potatoes and peas. It was good enough, though, and I finished it off with a big slab of apple pie. For a grown man I've got a terrible case of sweet tooth, though I seldom get a chance to satisfy it. When I was finished I ordered up two steaks to be put in a paper sack so I could take Chulo and Wilcey something to eat. While that was coming I settled back to read the paper. I went clean through it, and though there was reports of several killings over the last few days, there was none sounded as if it might have been done by the black *Meskin*.

I paid my score and left. On the way to the docks I stopped in a saloon and picked up a bottle of good brandy for my partners.

When I got to the docks, Wilcey was just about where I'd left him. He was hunkered up in the shade of the warehouse, smoking and looking bored.

"Anything happening?"

He shook his head. "Naw."

The docks were busy, with bunches of men loading and unloading ships. I'd been worried that we might have been conspicuous sitting there so long, but there were other bystanders watching the work.

I handed him the food and the bottle of brandy and he said, "Thank God. I was hoping you'd think on this. I was starting to get damned hungry."

"What's Nigger doing?"

He shook his head. "Sleeping probably. I ain't seen hide nor hair of him."

"Well, how you doing?"

"I'm okay. Plenty tired of sitting here. But, what the hell."

"Well, we've got to get horses. You want to go buy them and I'll stay and watch?"

He shook his head. "No. You're better at the kind of horses we need. I buy the wrong kind and I'd never hear the last of it."

"Now you know that ain't so."

"Just say I don't want to take the chance."

"All right. But I give you a choice."

It was coming one o'clock, a good five more hours before dark. Now that the sun was up good it had commenced to get hot, though the breeze blowing in off the water helped some.

I said: "Well, I don't know how long all this will take. I guess you'll see me when I get here."

"Take your time. Take your time. We'll be right here. Except I am beginning to feel like doing murder to that goddamn *Meskin*. I hope it's hot as hell down in that little cabin and he ain't able to sleep."

"Don't bet on it," I said, "I've seen that sonofabitch asleep on the desert with a cactus bush for a pillow. That bastard could sleep in the middle of a cattle stampede."

I left and went on downtown to look for the horses.

I went to several livery stables and horse barns, and it wasn't long before I figured out that Galveston was not the place to buy the kind of horses we needed. Men in our profession need horses that are rock hard and that have good early speed and that are stayers. Truly a horse, in our line of work, can mean the difference between capture and death or freedom.

In Galveston they had pretty horses, and nice-colored horses, and clean-limbed horses, but they didn't have no horses that was suitable for outlaws.

But we had to have horses so I finally bought three geldings, all around five years of age and all around sixteen hands high. They were nice horses, good and gentle, and I'm sure they were meant for the best and would have been fine for ladies and little kids to ride around Galveston, but they was city soft and would be very unused to the owl hoot trail. But then it wasn't but about sixty miles to Houston, and I figured they could make that, if we didn't get pursued. I'd had to give a hundred dollars apiece for them, but I figured that once we got to Houston I'd sell them at a loss and get us some horses we could do business on.

After I'd bought them I led them to a livery stable near our hotel and had the man give them a bait of corn and water them good and in general get them ready for a hard ride. Then I gave two boys there fifty cents each to come back over to the hotel with me and help lug all our saddles and gear back to the stable.

Our score was paid at the hotel for several days so there was no need to worry about that, and I'd get our money out of the safe as my last act before we left town. It was near four o'clock by the time I finished all that.

Outside of the hotel I stood debating. I knew I really ought to go back and relieve Wilcey and let him get out and around a little, but, hell, a couple more hours wasn't going to kill him. So, in the end, my baser nature won out and I walked down the street to the whorehouse where Marianne worked. The doors was open and there was a little crowd drinking, but none of the women were down. I got up to the bar and got a drink of brandy and stood there wondering who I could ask about Marianne. Finally, I motioned the bartender over and asked him when the girls was due. He just shrugged and said, "Oh, couple of hours more than likely. Most of them are still sleeping."

Hell, I didn't have a couple of hours. I spun a five-dollar gold piece on the bar and wondered if he could get word to the one called Marianne that I was here and my time was short. "Tell her it's the one she called cowboy last night."

I half expected him to make some wiseacre remark, but he just took the gold coin and said he'd see what could be done. Then he went out the other end of the bar and up the stairs.

I stood there nervous, wondering if she'd come down. And wasn't that a pretty come to pass! Standing there like some lovesick swain waiting on a whore! A whore, mind you.

But I couldn't help remembering how soft and white and sweet she'd been the night before. Maybe people don't know it, but the harder a man is the softer he likes his women. Even a hard man needs him a tender place to rest in every once in a while.

He was back in about two minutes, taking his own good time making his way down to my end of the bar. Then he said: "She says for you to come on up. But give her a few more minutes. It's the third door on the right off the top of the stairs."

I thanked him and ordered a bottle of brandy to take with me. Then I stood there, slowly sipping my way through three drinks figuring enough time had passed to make it seemly for me to go up.

Now ain't that something. You'd think she was the Queen of the May, the way I was treating her.

Finally I pushed away from the bar and went up the stairs, carrying my bottle of brandy. I knocked on the third door on the right and she cracked it enough to see out. Then she recognized me. "Oh, it's the Texan that saved me from all them goddamn furriners." She laughed and held the door open and I went in.

She was wearing some kind of lavender silk robe that was gaping open at the top so I could see most of her breasts. "Goddamn," she said, "I asked you to come early, but not this early."

"I'm leaving town," I said. "It was now or never."

I found a chair and did like I always did in every hotel room or whorehouse room I was in, took the chair and propped it under the doorknob so it wouldn't come open so easy.

She was taking off her robe and watching me. "I noticed you done that last night. How come?"

"Just habit," I said. I looked at her where she stood and she was just as I'd remembered. She was fair and a little plump. She had some small folds around her stomach, and her breasts were round and her hips well padded. To me she was beautiful. Looking at her I could feel my neck getting thick. I sat down on the side of the bed and undressed as fast as I could.

Then, for a good little while, all I did was lay beside her, feeling her softness, stroking her, kissing her, while she caressed me. Usually whores will hurry you, but she never had treated me like a customer and she seemed just as content to lay there.

Finally, when I could stand it no longer, I tried to bury myself in her again, thrusting into her as deep as I could, thrusting as if I were looking to tap some source for myself. When it was over I lay on top of her, trembling like a leaf in a high wind while she held me with soft arms and soothed me with soft hands.

After a time I rolled off her and then laid near her side. Which was very unusual for me. Mostly, after I've had a woman, I just want to get up and put my clothes on. But this time I was content to lay there and feel her smooth warm skin against my old rough hide.

I turned on my back and lit a cigarillo. She put her hand on my chest, rubbing it lightly. She said: "Who the hell are you?"

"I told you last night. My name is Jim."

She laughed lightly. "Jim what?"

"Jim Wilson."

"What do you do, Mister Wilson?"

I said, "Oh, I buy and sell cattle." Which was one of the answers I usually gave. That or a horse rancher.

She laughed again. "Whose cattle—yours or someone else's?"

"That's a hell of a thing to say to a man."

"Listen, sweetie." She raised up on one elbow and began touching the bullet-wound scars around my body, finding with her finger the two under my collarbone, the one in my shoulder, the one in my side, and the two in my thigh. "You didn't get those from singing too loud in Sunday school."

I said: "I got those in the war."

"What war?"

"Oh, the Civil War."

She laughed. "Don't hand me that. You'd of been about ten years old when the Civil War was over. If you was that old."

"I'm older than I look," I said.

"How come you're leaving so soon. God, I hate to say it, but I'm kinda disappointed."

"It's time to go," I said.

She kind of raised up where she could look me in the face. "Where you and that big gun you wear going?"

I shrugged and sat up. "Oh, north, I reckon."

"What you going to do with that big gun? Do you use it to make your living?"

"God, you're a curious woman." I got up off the bed and went over and looked out the window. It was coming twilight and I figured I'd better get in a hurry. But for some reason I was having a hard time leaving. Which didn't make a bit of sense. I'd done my business and now it was time to go. I pulled on my britches, then sat down in a chair and started pulling on my boots.

From the bed she asked: "You coming back tonight?"

I shook my head. "Naw. I'll be long gone."

"Hell," she said, "want to hear something stupid?"

"What?"

"I don't like the idea that I might never see you again. Ain't that a hell of a thing for a damn whore to be thinking."

I was silent for a moment. I should have been putting on my shirt, but, instead, I reached over and poured me a glass full of brandy and sat there sipping at it. Finally, I said: "You don't seem like a whore to me." Then I set the brandy down, reached and got my shirt, and started putting it on.

She didn't reply to what I'd said, just lay there looking at me.

I said: "Maybe I'll send for you. Send you a telegram."

"Sure you will. Don't make me laugh."

"I might. But you wouldn't come. So I guess I won't." I was buttoning my shirt.

"Sure I would," she said. Then she suddenly

laughed. "You know, it's funny, but I might really come. Wouldn't that be a joke on me."

I stood up and started strapping on my gun belt. "Why would you come? Why would you even think about it?"

"I don't know," she said. "You're a damned good-looking man. And you are a man." She paused. "No, that's not all it. Maybe—maybe it's because you don't treat me like a whore. You said that a while ago and it kind of hit me. I didn't feel like a whore with you."

I hesitated, feeling like a damn fool. "Where would I get word to you? That is if I was crazy enough to believe a telegram from me wouldn't do anymore than make you laugh."

"Here," she said. "The New Palace Saloon."

"Just to Marianne?"

"That'll reach me."

"Ain't you got a last name?"

"Yeah, but I don't want these jerks around here to know it."

"You care if I do?"

She hesitated and then said: "No. It's Mason."

"Marianne Mason. Nice name." I took a twenty-dollar gold piece out of my pocket and laid it on top of the bureau.

She said: "I ain't even sure if I want you to do that."

"Don't be loco. You may never see me again and twenty dollars is twenty dollars." I walked over and kissed her lightly on the lips. Then I put on my hat. "I got to go."

She said: "What do you really do? You spend money too freely for a cattleman. I'm from Oklahoma and I know how tight them bastards are."

I walked over and took the chair away from the door. "You really want me to tell you?"

"Yes."

"What will you do with it if I do?"

"Nothing."

"I'd be trusting you. I don't trust a lot of people."

"I don't reckon you do. You going to tell me?"

I gave her a half grin. "If I do you might not be willing to come to me if I sent for you. Not that you would anyway."

She said: "Do you know how crazy this sounds? You've fucked me twice and you're talking about sending for me and goddamnit, I'm not laughing. That's what's crazy."

"Maybe it is." I walked back over and kissed her lightly on the lips. "Good-bye, Marianne. Don't be surprised if you hear from me."

She slung her arm around my neck and kissed me back, hard. Then I pulled away and walked to the door. Just before I opened it I said: "I'm a bank robber."

She said: "I figured as much. Not that I knew you robbed banks. I just figured you was an outlaw of some kind."

"That make you think less of me?"

"Hell no! What the hell you think people think of me? Good-bye Jim Wilson."

I said: "That ain't really my name. But I won't tell you the real one just yet. If we ever see each other again I will. Good-bye."

Then I opened the door and went on out it, closing it behind me. As I was going down the stairs, I heard a door open behind me, and I looked back to see her standing just so she could look after me. I waved and she waved back and then I went on down the stairs and out the door.

It was coming dark and I felt a little bad about having had my pleasure while Wilcey had stood his lonely guard.

But I was glad I had.

Nevertheless, I wanted to hurry. I went straight to the livery stable, got the liveryman to help me saddle and bridle all three horses, then mounted one, took the other two on lead, and went to the hotel to get our money. I tied the horses in front and then clumped on in and went up to the desk. I had the receipt he'd given me, and I asked the clerk for all our money. To my surprise he said I could have mine, but that I could not take the money of the others.

I said: "Hell, they sent me for it. We're in a hurry."

He shook his head. "Sorry, gent. We don't know they did. And they got receipts which they'll have to hand in in person. We only give each one his belongings. Meaning no offense, but we're a reputable establishment and we mean to stay that way. No funny business here."

Well, I seen he wouldn't budge so I took my money, packed it in my saddlebags, and then mounted up and started for the docks. The hell of it was that it meant we'd have to bring Chulo back in to town when I'd figured all we'd have to do was get him off that boat and ride out of town.

I got to the warehouse, circled around one end until I was near to the edge of the dock, then dismounted and tied the horses to a handy post. I hoped everything was all right, but I wasn't sure until I come around the end of the warehouse and seen Wilcey pacing back and forth. I come up to him. "Everything all right?"

"Hell yes. Where the hell you been?"

"Been busy," I said. "Get Chulo. I got the horses at the end of the warehouse."

"What took you so damn long? It's been dark a good hour."

"Goddamnit, Wilcey. I had a lot to do. Now will

you go and get Chulo? I'm going back to the horses. Hurry."

"Now you want to hurry," he said disgustedly. But he started toward the boat while I went around the end of the warehouse and untied the horses. Well, he took so long that I finally got impatient and lit a cigarillo. But I was feeling so guilty about having taken that two hours with Marianne I didn't figure I'd better say anything.

Finally he come around the end of the building, but without Chulo. My heart sank.

I said: "What the hell! Where's the *Meskin*? Have you let him slip off into town?"

"Will, he's sick. He's seasick. I never seen it, but I've heard about it. Especially on that steamer we come over on."

"He's *what*!"

"He's seasick. He's laid there in that little close cabin with it rocking around, and now he's so damn sick he can't even stand up. My God, he looks like he's thrown up his asshole. The goddamn cabin smells like a pigsty."

"Oh, shit!" I said. "Of all the goddamn—" I stopped. There wasn't any use cussing about it. I said: "Can't you help him up and out?"

"Hell no! He's limp as a spent dick. You got to come help me."

"Damn!" I re-tied the horses and then followed him on board the little boat. The cabin door was still open, and I followed him down the two or three steps into the little cabin. Wilcey was sure right. The place smelled like hell and the floor was slippery with vomit. Chulo was laying on the bunk, moaning. I'd brought a bottle of brandy with me. I told Wilcey, "Let's get him set up right and get some of this down him."

Well, we sat him up straight and he was so weak

that he was wobbling. But Wilcey held his head while I poured some of the brandy down him.

It wasn't but a minute before we seen that was a mistake.

Wilcey said: "Goddamn, Will, we got to get him up in the fresh air. It's so close down here I'm about to get sick."

"Yeah, you're right," I said.

We struggled him upright and about half drug, half carried him up the little steps. God, he was a mess and, as limp as he was, seemed to weigh about the same as a full-grown steer.

But we finally got him up on deck. I said: "Let's get him to the horses."

The fresh air seemed to revive him a little, and he was able to walk some, though we still had to help him. We nearly lost him in to the water getting from the boat to the dock, but in the end we had him upright on land. We let him stand a moment, getting his bearings. He still hadn't said a word, just moaned.

Finally we walked him around to the horses. "Let's get him on this one," I said. But the horse shied back, smelling Chulo. Hell, I didn't blame the horse.

It took us several tries, but we finally got him in the saddle. While Wilcey held him from the ground I swung up on my mount. Then I reached over and slapped the *Meskin* hard in the face.

He just moaned. "I seck. I seck."

"I know you're seck, you sonofabitch. But you can't be sick."

"I wan' to go asleepe."

"No." I slapped him again. "We got to get out of here and you got to gather yourself up. You hear me! Goddamnit!"

"Oh, Weelson," he said. "I seck!"

"Fuck you." I held out the bottle of brandy. "Now

you take this and try and get a drink down. Maybe it'll settle your stomach."

While Wilcey continued to hold him in the saddle, he reached out with two unsteady hands and took the bottle. It took him a couple of tries to lift it to his mouth, but he finally was able to take a long pull. He handed me the bottle back and we watched anxiously, hoping for some improvement.

Again it was a mistake.

"I ain't standing near that sonofabitch again," Wilcey said disgustedly.

I threw up my hands. "I don't know what the hell to do. Have you got any idea what to give somebody that's seasick?"

Wilcey just shook his head.

I said: "Well, we got to do something. We got to get out of here and quick. But we couldn't make a mile, sick's this sonofabitch is. I tell you. This is a sea town. Got to be someone around here knows what to do. You mount up and hold this bastard in the saddle while I go and see if I can find somebody to tell us what to do."

He mounted and took hold of Chulo, who was weaving back and forth in the saddle, and I turned my horse away and rode out to the front of the warehouse to look for any help I could find. Down around one of the gaslights, about a hundred yards away, I could see a man standing, looking out to sea. I rode toward him hoping he wouldn't be one of them foreign sailors who couldn't speak English.

He looked a little startled when I come pulling up beside him. I said, "Are you from around here?"

He looked more like one of the townspeople rather than a sailor. He gave me a long look.

"Why you asking?"

I said, "Me and my partner are not from this part

of the country. And we don't know nothing about boats or that kind of stuff. Do you?"

"A little," he said, still watching me carefully.

I said: "Well, the truth of it is, my partner's seasick, mortal seasick, and I don't know what to give him. You got any ideas?"

He looked at me a long moment and then started to laugh.

I said: "Goddamnit, it ain't funny! We got a bunch of miles to make tonight and that bastard can't even sit a horse!"

He stopped laughing, but he was still smiling. He said: "Give him a good drink of vinegar."

"Of *what!*"

"Vinegar."

"You mean that stuff a woman uses in the kitchen?"

"The same. Give him a drink of that."

I had never heard of such a thing. Giving a man a drink of vinegar. I said: "But won't it make him sick?"

He said: "I thought you told me he was already sick."

"He is. Awful sick."

"Well, it won't make him any sicker. And it might work. Sometimes it does."

I thought. But then what the hell did I know about seasickness. I said: "But where am I supposed to get any vinegar at this time of night?"

He turned and pointed up the dockside. "See that light yonder? That's a ship chandler's. Likely he'll have some."

I said, "Well, thanks. We'll give it a try." I put spurs to my horse and loped on up the waterfront. Sure enough it was a ship's store and they were open. I dismounted and went inside and they did have vinegar. I bought a little bottle, remounted, and rode back toward the warehouse, waving at the stranger as I passed.

Wilcey and Chulo were just about in the same position when I come riding up—Chulo reeling in the saddle and Wilcey holding him as steady as he could. I asked: "He any better?"

Wilcey shrugged. "Depends on what you mean by better. He ain't throwed up no more, but then I reckon he's already fetched it all. What's that you got there?"

I said: "I'll tell you if it works." I took Chulo by the shoulder and shook him. "Listen, Nigger, I'm going to give you a little bottle and I want you to take a drink of it. You understand?"

Wilcey said, alarm in his voice, "Goddamn, Will, not too much! I don't want to get sprayed again."

I said, "All right." And to Chulo, as I uncapped the bottle and handed it to him, "Here. Just take a little drink for right now."

"I seeck," he said. "I wan' lie down."

I shook him again. "Goddamnit! Take this bottle and take a little drink or I'll kill your sorry ass!"

He took the bottle and raised it to his lips, but hesitated.

"Drink it!" I commanded.

He took a little sip and immediately spat it out.

"Goddamn you, Chulo!" I swore. "Drink it! We got no more time!"

"It taste like sheet," he said weakly.

"How you know? You ever eat shit? Now you drink it or so help me I'll throw you on the ground and pour it down your throat!"

He put the bottle to his mouth, took a quick little drink, and swallowed.

We watched him expectantly. After a minute had passed and it had stayed down, I commanded him to take another. He did, a longer one this time, shuddering as he swallowed.

But it stayed down.

"More," I said, after a moment.

He took another drink and we sat there watching him expectantly. I tell you it was the damndest change I've ever seen. When we'd first brought him up from that cabin and got him in the light the black Mexican was so pale I thought he'd turned white. But now some color was starting to come back in his face and he wasn't weaving around anymore. He was beginning to look like his old self.

"Chico," I said, "how you feel?"

He shook himself, like a dog shedding a load of water. He said: "Not so bad, *amigo*."

"You think you can ride?"

"Chure. Chulo can always ride. What the hell you theenk?"

Wilcey asked me: "What the hell was that stuff?"

"Vinegar," I said. "But don't tell Chulo. Now let's get out of here."

We rode out around the warehouse, and I stopped them and told both about the money in the hotel safe.

Wilcey said, "Aw, hell! We ain't never going to get out of this goddamn town!"

I said: "Well, what's our selection?"

He said: "Don't look like we got one. Onliest thing to do is me and Chulo to walk in to that goddamn hotel and claim our money. Likely the high sheriff will be sitting right there."

"Don't give up yet, old woman," I said. "They's a public watering trough right up here. Let's take a stop there and see if we can get the Nigger cleaned up just a little."

We rode on up there and dismounted. I looked through Chulo's saddlebags and come out with one of

his shirts. I was damned if I was going to use one of
mine. Then I dipped it in the water and scrubbed off
his front as best I could. God, he was a mess! And
smelled to high heaven. I done the best I could, but
all I did was make him look like he'd fell in a creek.

I said: "That's the best I can do. We'll just have to
make out as well as we can."

Chulo was pretty docile. I reckon he was still a
little weak. Riding over to the hotel he said: "I
plenty *hambre*." I'm hungry.

I said: "Be goddamned if I care how hungry you
are. You're going in that hotel so you and Wilcey can
get your money, and you're going to keep your goddamn mouth shut. You hear me, *Meskin!*"

He said mildly, "Why you get so angry, Weelson? I
steel your *amigo*."

"Aw, shit!" I said.

We pulled up in front of the hotel and Wilcey and
Chulo got down. I was plenty nervous. They was just
going in to get their own money out of the safe, but I
was as jumpy as if they was going in to rob the goddamn place and I was waiting outside holding the
horses.

I told Wilcey: "Make this as fast as you can. I want
out of this downtown area."

He gave me a sour look. "You're preaching to the
choir, partner."

They handed me their reins and went on in. The
desk was a little to the back, and I couldn't see them
through the window. Sitting my horse, I looked
around nervously, expecting law along at any moment. The streets, as usual, were crowded. I sat my
horse, waiting for them to come back, wondering
what the hell was taking them so long.

Finally, just as I was considering going in and
seeing what the hell was, they come out.

"They took long enough," I said. "Ya'll stop in the bar for a drink?"

Wilcey gave me one of his sour looks. "The *Meskin* couldn't find his receipt. I finally found it in his hatband."

"Enough of this," I said. "Let's make some tracks."

Galveston is an island, and we had to cross the bay on what they call a causeway, which is a hellaciously long wooden bridge. I tell you, I was glad to find out about the causeway, it being the only way out of town. It convinced me they wasn't going to have much robbery in that town, not if they wasn't but one way to make your getaway.

But we clumped over it, our horses' hooves sounding hollow and loud on the boards of the bridge.

Chulo seemed to be just about himself again, though he kept complaining of being hungry. I reckon he was. I reckoned he throwed up everything except his toenails.

I handed him the bottle of brandy. "Here," I said, "suck on this. Because we ain't going to be stopping at no cafés."

We got off the bridge and hit the road. It was a dark night with little moon, and now that the sun was down it had turned cool, what with the sea breeze.

Wilcey said: "I feel a hell of a long way off my range."

I said: "I know what you mean."

Chapter Three

We rode a considerable way that night, mainly because it was so dark we couldn't see good enough to find a campsite. We rode off the road a few times, but we kept running into marshy land that sunk our horses' hooves up to their hocks.

Finally, after about six hours in the saddle, with them soft city horses about to give out on us, we found a little rise with a clump of oak trees fronting it. We pulled in there, got down, got unsaddled, picketed the horses, and built a little fire. We didn't have any food. In the rush to get away none of us had thought of it. But we did have a little coffee left in our saddlebags, and we brewed up a pot of that, laced our cups with brandy, and then sat around the fire, leaned back against our saddles, and sort of cooled out.

I wasn't too worried about pursuit. I didn't figure they had much of a line on Chulo, and I was about to begin to figure they had so many killings in that town among all them foreigners that nobody paid much attention.

I was just glad Chulo hadn't killed a townsperson, for I figured they treated that a little different, and I told him as much.

He said: "I don' theenk I ever keel nobody again.

Not if I got to hide on a goddamn boat. I rather they hang me."

After a time we turned in to our blankets. We was all plenty tired. But for a time I laid there, looking up at the dark sky, and thought about Marianne.

It didn't make a damn bit of sense, me laying there thinking about a whore. God knows I'd never done that before. Yet there I lay, her on my mind.

Well, it was true what I'd told her: that I didn't feel like she was a whore. Maybe if things had been different, maybe if I hadn't still had a few lingering thoughts on my mind about that little senorita Linda it wouldn't have been the same. Maybe it was just that I was needing and wanting a woman so bad.

But I didn't really think that was it. For she had seemed to feel the same about me.

I tell you what was part of the proof and that was that I'd kissed her on the mouth and she'd let me. She'd even kissed me back.

And whores don't do that.

I'd learned that a long time ago. To them there's a difference between fucking and kissing. Fucking is business and that's all right. But kissing is personal and they don't give that out to everyone. It's got to be that special someone.

And then there was the business about me saying, even kidding at first, that I might send for her. And her saying she might come.

Hell, like she'd said, that was crazy. Just damn crazy. A man didn't talk to a whore like that and she didn't answer him like that.

But, goddamn me, damned if I wasn't thinking about it.

Now, how's that for just plain out and out crazy?

I went to sleep that night thinking about her warm, soft, white body and her pretty face that seemed to get prettier every time I thought of her.

We stirred awake the next morning in the midst of a fog bank. It was kind of a strange sight, us moving around trying to make a fire and have a little coffee, with each man looking like he was wandering around waist-deep in water. And when a man would bend over to try and rustle up some wood, it would look as if he'd gone clean under.

Wilcey said in disgust, "Goddamn, don't the sun ever shine in this country?"

"It's just now up," I said. "It'll burn off here directly."

We finally got a fire going, and I made coffee while Wilcey and Chulo got up the horses and got them bridled and saddled. The fire burned away the fog in a little circle around it, otherwise we'd have all looked like we was sitting in a cloud.

The coffee finally boiled and we poured up our cups, adding the regular amount of brandy, and then sat around trying to get waked up good. None of us had really had enough sleep, except Chulo, but that's one of the hazards of the outlaw trade. Chulo said he still felt a little weak, and I figured he would until he got some food in his belly.

But, for that matter, we was all plenty hungry.

Wilcey said: "Don't seem to make much sense. Here we sit with better'n twenty thousand dollars between us and yet we all got empty bellies. Well, just goes to prove money ain't everything."

"No," I said, "but it's damn close. We'll be in Houston by early afternoon, and then I reckon you'll be glad you got money in your pocket for we'll have us the best meal that money can buy. And ain't ever'body can make that statement."

"You figured out yet what we going to do when we get there?"

"You mean what kind of business we are going to do?"

"Yeah, what else?"

"Well, hell, Wilcey, wait until we get there first. I ain't never even been to Houston before."

He said, "Huh! Never seen that stop you before. We pulled that bank robbery in Sabinas Hidalgo without you knowing a hell of a lot about it."

"Wilcey, I had spent considerable amount of time in Sabinas."

"But you planned that bank robbery without so much as even going in the bank."

"Aw, hell," I said, "sometimes you piss me off."

He give me that sardonic grin and I seen the sonofabitch had been carrying me. He's always doing that to me and I'm always fool enough to fall for it. And it's goddamn seldom I can catch him that same way.

We had another cup and then killed the fire and put the gear away and mounted up.

There was already some wagon traffic on the road and now and again a few horsemen, either alone or in pairs. It was a good road and I imagine there was a good deal of commerce between the two cities, Galveston being the biggest port and Houston being the biggest city in Texas. I'd been told you could get damn near anything you wanted in Houston.

The sun got up and it got humid. It bothered Chulo and Wilcey some, but I was still kind of used to it, having grown up down in that coastal country around Corpus Christi.

Of course it gave Wilcey something else to complain about "this goddamn country." But he'd already made it clear he was anxious to be back on our border range, so he'd been complaining no matter where he was. I finally told him to shut up, just to content himself with his lot for the time being.

We seen Houston a good ways off before we got to it, even in that flatland country with no hills to get a good view off of. It just come rising up out of the prairie when we was still a good three or four miles out.

"Lord," Wilcey said, "look at them buildings!"

They were tall. I bet there was some six or eight stories high, maybe even higher.

We kept right on, and pretty soon we were clattering through the outskirts, still a good ways from what appeared to be the downtown section.

"God, it's big, ain't it?" I said.

Wilcey said: "I can't for the life of me understand why people in their right minds would want to live all jammed up like this. God damn, they ain't room to breathe here."

Then pretty soon we were in amongst all those tall buildings. The streets were wide and not too muddy, but the entire place was just working alive with buggies and wagons and men on horseback and afoot and everybody hurrying and scurrying like a schoolboy late to dinner.

I give it a good looking over as we went ambling along. Finally I said, "Gentlemen, it appears there's a power of money in this place and some of it belongs to us."

Wilcey said: "We'd be better off heading for Texas."

I said: "You idiot, this is Texas. Hell, don't you know anything."

But he shook his head. "No, this ain't Texas. Maybe it's you never seen Texas. This don't look a thing like Texas. This looks like pictures of them Yankee cities I've seen in newspapers."

"All right," I said, "all right. We know you ain't happy here. But for right now lets get settled in and get something to eat."

I managed to slow one of them fast-walking townspeople down long enough to ask him where a good hotel was. He give us a looking over, probably noting how travel worn we were, and I figured he was fixing to recommend some sleazy joint so I told him price wasn't no object. He shrugged and said there was a number of good ones and he reckoned the Texas Hotel was as good as any.

Well, it was but a few blocks down the street and we cantered on down there. The hotel even had its own livery stable so we turned our horses in there, even leaving our saddles, which the stable man gave me to understand was the custom in such stylish hotels.

We took two rooms, me and Wilcey bunking together as was our habit. We didn't do it because Chulo was a *Meskin* or snored or anything. We done it because Chulo had the habit of coming in at three or four in the morning dragging the god-awfulest alley cat you could imagine. Where he found some of those women and how they got in the condition they were always in just beat the hell out of me. I'd bunked in with him a few times, and you never heard such moaning and groaning and screaming and yelling in all your life. He was always sorry the next day that he'd interrupted your sleep, but at the time he didn't give a damn.

This was a pretty swanky hotel, with marble columns in the lobby and carpet on the floor, and they even said there was a bathhouse on each and every floor and that you didn't have to book a bath in advance, but could just go and take one providing there wasn't anyone there ahead of you.

We were all on the fourth floor and I was commenting on all of that as we climbed the stairs. Wilcey said: "They ought to have all this stuff. Four dollars a day! Just for a place to lay your head! Goddamn, we think we're robbers! Shit, they ought to get 'em a gun and do it honestly."

That kind of talk from a man who had nearly eight thousand dollars.

We got to the room and got settled in. Chulo came over from his room and I asked what everybody wanted to do. Did they want to get a bath first, or go get something to eat? Wilcey and I were both for taking a bath, but Chulo declared he would be *"morte"* damn quick if he didn't get something to eat.

Well, he had a point. "Besides," I said, "it's a little early to go out and look the town over. So let's eat now and then we can come back and get a little of this farming land off and go out and do a little serious drinking."

The clerk told us the best eating establishment in town was right next door, place called Delmonico's, so we went in there. Lord, it was plenty elegant. The chairs were padded and they had a cloth on the table; they even had a chandelier. I reckoned we looked a little out of place in such an establishment, though I'd been glad to note, as we come in to town, that we weren't going to look as out of place, as a general thing, in Houston as we had in Galveston. Most folks were dressed like city people, in shoes and broadcloth suits and derby hats, but there was still a good number of hombres around dressed like we were, most of them carrying guns.

They had something on the menu I hadn't seen in a long time, raw oysters. I hadn't eaten them all that often, but, being from near the coastal country, I was familiar with them, so I ordered up a batch along with a steak and some other stuff. Chulo said he thought he'd try some too, but Wilcey, being from West Texas and never having heard of them, said he'd just wait and see what they looked like. When they came he took one look and said they were the nastiest things he'd ever seen and any man that would put such a thing in his mouth would damn near eat anything.

But one thing we all enjoyed was the cold beer they had. I didn't know how long it had been since I'd had cold beer, but they told me it was all over town, that they had ice-making machinery there and that ice was the cheapest thing around. Well, all that was doing was convincing me more and more that there was a lot of money in Houston. Now all I had to do was to figure out how we could get our hands on some and make a good getaway.

I didn't think it was going to be easy. I'd never done robbery in such a big place, and I wasn't sure how a man could go about it. Making a getaway might be the hardest part, for it would be a long ride before a man even hit the open prairie where he'd have a running chance to get away from any chase party that might be in pursuit. And the idea of being hemmed in by all them buildings while God knows who might be shooting at you wasn't a thing I wanted to get involved with.

We got done eating and Wilcey and Chulo went on back to the hotel to get cleaned up. I wanted some new shirts and britches. I didn't see no point in taking a bath and then putting back on them same clothes I'd practically been living in for the last two weeks. I found me a haberdashery down the street and went in and bought two new pair of pants and three new shirts and some new socks. The salesman tried to interest me in what he called "undergarments," but I didn't tell him what I thought of men who wore such things.

By the time I got back to the room Wilcey had had his bath and Chulo was in there.

"How does it work?" I asked him. "The boy bring up buckets of water like they do down on the border?"

He shook his head. "Naw. They got a big overhead tank in there and you pull a lever and it comes running out. You get cold out of one and hot out of the other. Then, when you're finished, you pull a plug and all your water runs out of the tub so that the next man gets clean."

He was sitting on his bunk drinking brandy straight out of the bottle. I sat down on mine, which was on the other side of the room. He pitched me the bottle and I had a light pull.

"What do you think so far?" he asked me.

I shook my head. "I don't know, Dennis. It's mighty big. Let's just bide our time until we see the right chance. We got plenty of money and I don't see no need to rush."

He said: "From what I've seen there appears to be plenty of law around here. I'd heard about uniformed policemen. Did you take note of that one on the street near the café? In his blue uniform and hat?"

"Yeah, I saw him. But, Dennis, there's going to be law looking for us anywhere we go. I just don't think they're going to be looking for us here. Hell, why should they? I may be wrong, but I feel kind of safe here."

Which was true. As big as the place was it give me the feeling that a man could get lost in it. Of course, that was just a guess on my part, but then that's what I'd been doing all my life, guessing and gambling.

Chulo come in and I gathered up a new shirt and a new pair of pants and went on down to the bathroom. It was just as Wilcey had said it would be. I undressed and put my new clothes on a little stool and threw my old ones in the corner. I was just going to leave them there. I figured they'd done their duty long enough and anybody that wanted them could have them. Then I put my pistol on top of my clothes and my hat on top of that and pushed the stool over next to the big, galvanized tub.

Well, it taken me a minute to get the levers straightened out. First I got it too cold, then too hot, but pretty soon it come out to where I wanted and I climbed in and, my, didn't it feel good.

I laid there in that warm, clean water, smoking a cigarillo and feeling mighty good. Only thing I was regretting was I'd forgotten to bring me a bottle of cognac. That would just about have topped it off.

Hell, it wasn't a good life, the owl hoot trail, but there was some good moments. Moments like I'd had with Marianne, and moments like I was having now. But it didn't really matter since it looked as if it was going to be my life the rest of my days. I figured all I could do was make the best of it. My mind turned back a number of years, back to when I was about twenty and had been an outlaw for about three years. I'd made my way back to the little town that was near our ranch outside of Corpus. My daddy was dead then, killed by the loss of all he'd worked so long to build up, and my mother had followed him shortly, of a broken heart I reckoned. But I'd still had an old maid aunt living there, a schoolteacher, and I slipped into town, a wanted man, to see her and what few friends I had left there. I'd gone in to her neat and tidy little parlor with its doilies on the chair arms and knickknacks scattered all over and let myself gingerly down in one of them chairs she had that never seemed so much for sitting as for being looked at. And she'd sat across from me, her hands folded in her lap, her mouth so set and sour, and said: "Well, I see you've gone bad, Wilson. I could have predicted it."

I guess she'd made such a success out of her own life that she was set up to sit in judgment of me.

No matter, her words had hurt me, for I'd never

meant to become an outlaw, but just had drifted into it and then had spent so many years just trying to pull off that last robbery that would gain me the money to buy respectability and the home that I'd always wanted.

That, as I've said, was all behind me now. The last robbery I'd ever pull would be the one they killed me on. And if they never killed me, then I'd die of old age pulling the last one.

Laying there in that warm water I thought of something that Marianne had said that first night when we were laying together in the early-morning hours just before I'd left. She'd said: "Hell, I don't mind being a whore. It's other folks that seem to take such a low view of it."

Which was true. I didn't mind being a robber. It was just that other people was so down on it.

I was ruminating over these things when the door suddenly opened. Without pause my hand went in under my hat and outed with my big pistol, cocking it as I drew it free and pointing it at the door.

Nearly scaring a young black boy who was bringing in some fresh towels to death.

He said, "Mighty sorry, suh! Mighty sorry!"

You never seen anybody set towels down and get out of a bathroom so fast in all your life.

When he was gone I had to laugh for about a minute. Here was the bad Wilson Young, feared by a lot of men, nearly about to shoot a towel boy.

Well, it was about time to get out so I let out the water, toweled off, put on my new clothes, and went back to the room. Hell, I was feeling fine. In the room Wilcey was still sitting on his bunk drinking brandy, and Chulo had him a chair pulled up to the window and was staring out at the city.

It was just coming dark and you've never seen such a power of lights in all your life. I'd thought that

Galveston was a lit-up city, but it wouldn't hold a candle to this Houston.

We went on out after a while. Enough time had passed so that we was hungry again so we stopped in at this Delmonico's and put on another feed. I ate fried chicken this time, with hot biscuits and honey, and some vegetable on the side.

After that we went walking out to see what the town had to offer. We stopped into several saloons along this street, which was Texas Avenue and which seemed to be the main thoroughfare of the town.

The crowds we found in the different drinking establishments was about a mixture of townsfolk and folk dressed like us. I'd been given to understand that there was a good cattle industry around Houston, so I had good hope of finding us the kind of horses I was looking for. After a time Chulo wanted to go off and find a whorehouse. I told him that would be just fine, but I stopped him before he could leave. I said, and he knew I meant it, "Now, Nigger, I don't care how drunk or how crazy you get. I don't care who pulls a knife on you. Don't you get us into no trouble or you're going to have me to deal with. We've got to be around this place a pretty good little while so you watch your step."

"Aw, Weelson," he said, "Chulo don't make no trouble."

But he knew I meant it.

After he was gone me and Wilcey settled in to a pretty nice saloon called the Shamrock Bar. They had a roulette wheel out in the open and several poker games going on in the back. Wilcey had made his living for a good number of years as a gambler, as had I for several when I was out of partners and having to run on my own.

I nodded toward the back rooms. "Reckon we ought to go take a hand?"

He shook his head. "Aw, you go ahead. I think I'm going out and find me a woman. I kind of missed out in Galveston."

"You didn't get laid?"

"Just once," he said. "Nothing like what you and Chulo was doing."

He left and I went on back and found a seat in a medium-priced game. My luck wasn't nothing special, neither particularly bad nor particularly good. About midnight I started yawning and I cashed in, about forty dollars to the good, and went on back to the hotel and went to sleep. I was so tired that I didn't even bother to lay and think as I usually do.

Wilcey was still sleeping next morning when I got up. So I just got dressed and wandered out on the town. I had me a good breakfast, finishing it off with coffee and brandy, then got me a high-priced cigar and went out the door of the café feeling well pleased with the way the day was starting.

Mostly I just wandered around. I did buy me a new hat and I did stop in at a bootmaker's and order me a custom pair of shop-made boots. My old ones was near about give out, and I figured I owed myself a pair of the best boots I could have made.

I looked some horses over at various horse barns and livery stables and I found a few that I thought would serve, but I figured that since we weren't in any rush I'd just keep looking until I found exactly what was needed.

In the early afternoon I took a light lunch at a little café off the beaten path and then set out to look the local banks over.

It didn't take me long to realize there wasn't much doing in that direction. Every one of them suckers was all marble and bars and a lot of armed guards standing around with shotguns under their arms. There might be bandits who would take on one of those Houston banks, but I was not one of them.

Other than that I just kind of wandered the streets, looking at the people, having an occasional drink in a bar, and just in general kind of sizing the place up. Once I passed a telegraph office and I about half seriously thought of going in and sending Marianne a telegram just to see what would happen. But I figured that was a fool's play so I give that idea up pretty quick. Still, it didn't keep her off my mind. I don't know what a man needs with a woman so damn bad, but it's a fact that he does.

When I got back to the room, Wilcey was sitting there watching the city out the window and drinking a little tequila.

I sat down on the opposite bed. "Where'd you get the Mexican whiskey?"

"They sell it here," he said.

"I didn't think you liked it."

"Generally I don't. Guess I'm getting homesick."

I didn't say anything and he swung away from the window. "What you been doing?"

I told him. He said: "Well, what do you think so far?"

I shrugged. "I think we're a long way off our range. I think I ain't sure if I'd even know how to plan a robbery in such a place. I think I ain't even sure if a robbery can be successfully pulled off in this big city. I think I just don't know."

He said, "Then fuck it. Let's go home."

I snorted. "Where's home, Wilcey?"

"Anyplace but here."

I shook my head. "Naw, we ain't going to leave for a while. I want a little time to get the feel of this place. There's plenty of money here. I just ain't figured out a way to get our share yet."

He said: "Goddamn, Will! What's the point of

sticking around here butting our heads up against a gamble? We *know* what to do down along the border and in Mexico. We *know* how to do robbery down there. Hell, I ain't interested in going back to school. Let's get out of here and go find us a sure thing."

I looked at him. He sure didn't look happy. But I knew Wilcey well enough to know that he very seldom was happy. I said: "Listen, you remember not even a year ago when me and you was in that line cabin up on that ranch in the Panhandle? When we was waiting to rob that payroll? When it was so cold we had to keep a side of beef inside to keep it from freezing so hard we'd never have been able to hack a steak off it? When me and you had cabin fever so bad we damn near killed each other? When that wind whistled through them cracks so hard we damn near couldn't keep a candle burning? When we was so broke we couldn't of paid attention? You remember that?"

He kind of half nodded.

I said: "Well, I remember you vowing that if we ever got out of that mess and got a few dollars in our pockets again that you'd never complain no more. You remember saying that?"

He just gave me a kind of sour look.

I said: "So here we sit. We can drink and eat and smoke and fuck damn near anything we want. We're in the best lodging you or I ever had. We got money in our pocket and we're safe enough here we can walk around on the streets. Now when we were back in that line cabin, wouldn't you have traded for this at the drop of a hat?"

He looked away and wouldn't answer me. I said: "So you just shut up all that wanting-to-leave talk and take it easy and have yourself a good time. Now, throw me that bottle of tequila."

He pitched it over to me and I had a pull and

damn near gagged. I said, "Well, I goddamn well ain't homesick for this shit."

We sat in silence for a while and then I said: "How'd you make out with the girls last night?"

He looked at me. "You mean in the whorehouse? Hell, I got money and any man can get laid in a whorehouse if he's got enough money. At least he knows what he's getting for his money."

Oh, Wilcey was bitter about women all right. I'd heard him say, more than once, "Ain't but two kinds of women and both of them is whores. Only difference is with one you hand her the five dollars direct. The other kind you give the five dollars to the preacher. But the end is going to be the same. You'll get fucked either way."

I sometimes thought Wilcey's bitterness was some kind of protection for the hurt he still felt inside about what his wife had done to him. But I never had no words to make him feel any better. Reckon there wasn't anyone else that did either.

Chapter Four

∿∿∿∿∿∿∿∿∿∿∿∿∿∿∿∿∿∿∿∿∿∿∿∿∿

We'd been there about a week and nothing much had turned up in the way of business opportunities. Chulo had left for San Antonio about the fourth day saying, "I got to go fuck me some *Meskin* weemen. These women here no good for Chulo."

I'd said: "When did you get so choosy?"

I was to send him a telegram when we got ready to "rob one of the *chinga gringo bancos.*"

Of course I knew how to wire him at his cousin's in San Antonio. As a matter of fact his cousin's sister was one of the good women I'd let get away from me while I was mooning over the highborn little senorita down in Sabinas Hidalgo. She would have made a damn fine outlaw's wife. In fact, she'd been married to one until he got killed.

I spent most of my time just looking around, trying to find the right kind of chance where we might take a little of the money that belonged to us. Nothing was showing, however. At one point I considered robbing one of the gambling joints, but it looked too much like suicide to me. There were too many people around, it didn't appear to be that much money, and I couldn't figure out how we could make a getaway.

Nights I mostly spent drinking or playing a little low-stakes poker. I was getting rested up, so rested up that I was starting to get a little nervous. Laying around is all right for a time, but I didn't want to make a steady thing of it.

Wilcey had been acting strange, or at least he was to my mind. He'd taken up the habit of disappearing in the afternoon. We usually ate breakfast and then the noon meal together, but then he'd take off somewhere and wouldn't show up until late, and twice he didn't come in all night long.

What's more, he'd quit complaining about being in Houston. And to me that was the strangest thing of all. I didn't say nothing to him about it. Whatever he was doing was his business. He might have just been spending an awful lot of time in whorehouses, but I doubted it. That just wasn't Wilcey's style.

We continued to go unrecognized. Once a man had come up to me in a bar and wondered if he didn't know me. I'd tensed up, but he'd finally decided I wasn't the man he'd met in New Orleans.

Well, one thing had happened. I'd been walking by the telegraph office one day, and on impulse I'd ducked inside and sent Marianne a telegram. I didn't want to make it sound like I really meant anything by it for fear, I guess, of being high-hatted. So I just made up the kind of telegram that didn't mean nothing. I said:

AM HERE BUYING CATTLE. WONDERED IF A TELEGRAM REALLY WOULD REACH YOU. YOU CAN WIRE ME BACK AT THIS OFFICE. WILL BE HERE A FEW MORE DAYS.

I wasn't really expecting a reply, so it was a couple of days later before I even bothered to check at the hotel desk for any mail or messages. Only reason I did was that Wilcey had been out all night and I was getting ready to go to the noon meal and thought he might have tried to get word to me. But there in my little cubbyhole was a telegram. Not only that, but the clerk said it had come the day before.

So she'd wired me right back. I walked outside, tearing open the envelope. She'd wired:

THOUGHT YOUR TELEGRAM WAS TO ASK ME TO JOIN YOU. AM DISAP-POINTED. HOPE YOU ARE BUYING A LOT OF CATTLE.

Well, I was that surprised. Of course I still didn't know if she was serious, or if she was just treating it as a joke. Curiously, one thing I wasn't worried about was that she might be stringing me along to bring the law down on my head. For some reason I had not the slightest fear of that. I guess because she struck me as being about as much outlaw as me. But what in the world she'd want with someone like me was more than I could imagine. She was a damn high-priced whore, and she must have understood, from talking to me, that I had no intention of paying her for her company. If she come to join me, it would be strictly on her own. Oh, I'd treated her damn fine, but I sure as hell wasn't going to pay her wages.

I mulled it over in my mind for a couple of days and then composed another telegram as carefully as I could, composing it so there'd be no mistake on her part and yet not trying to leave myself too open should she be joking with me.

Oh, yes, I know I'm tough, but I've been hurt aplenty by women and I'd rather have a bullet wound than that kind of hurt.

I wired her back:

WILL BE HERE TWO MORE WEEKS.

WOULD YOU FEEL LIKE TAKING A VACA-
TION AND COMING TO ME?

I sent the telegram in the morning and her answer
came back that afternoon. She said:

YES. WHEN?

I had been walking around for two days with her
answer burning in my pocket. I was still not willing
to believe she'd come, and I didn't want to make a
fool out of myself. There was a train between Galveston and Houston, and I had gone so far as to check
the schedule. I kept thinking about it and kept thinking about it, and I finally decided that if she didn't
come I'd be the only one who knew I had egg on my
face and then I could just put her out of my mind
once and for all. Hell, she was just a damn whore, after all, and there was no use me acting like a silly
schoolboy over the likes of her.

Friday was three days away and I went down and
wired her:

COME FRIDAY. I WILL MEET THE NOON
TRAIN.

Well, now it was up to her. And I, for one, wasn't
going to worry about it. I'd meet the train but I was
prepared to be disappointed. Wasn't no more women
going to make a fool out of Wilson Young.

Wilcey was in the room when I got back from the
telegraph office. It was early afternoon. He was sitting
there drinking brandy and water. He'd bought him
some new clothes also and a new hat, and we'd both
taken to shaving every day and taking way more

baths than we were used to. We were becoming quite the dandies.

I took the bottle from him and poured some in a glass and then added water. He said: "What the hell you been up to?"

I went over and sat down on my bunk. "That's a hell of a question for you to ask me. I been wondering if you'd moved out."

He said: "Well, you seen anything so far we might be interested in?"

I shook my head and told him about the gambling joints. "I don't know, Wilcey. Might be we won't see nothing around here. We might just be taking us a vacation and not knowing it."

He said: "I'd just soon we were." Then he hesitated. "Though I ain't in no big hurry to leave. I'm kinda enjoying this."

I looked at him. "Well, this is a big change. What brought this about?"

"Aw, nothing," he said. Then he said, abruptly, "I might have seen something you'd be interested in. Ain't sure. Looks awful tough to me, but you might see it a different way."

"What?"

"Well, they got a cotton exchange here."

"What's that?"

"That's a place where they buy and sell cotton. I don't mean the actual cotton. They got that in a warehouse somewhere. It's a place where the buyers and sellers get together. Price changes all the time. And a good number of the trades are done in cash, so they keep plenty on hand."

"Wait a minute now. Is this sort of a market?"

"Something like that. It's in one of them big buildings down about three blocks on Texas Avenue."

"Is there many people down there?"

"Oh, hell yes. A regular crowd. And plenty of

guards. I ain't talking about stealing no money out of there. Hell, you'd need an army."

"Well, what are you talking about?"

He took a drink of brandy and water and said: "Well, sometimes the place runs short on cash so they bring some over from the bank, which is about two blocks away. Guy brings it in a sack with a couple of guards along."

"The hell you say!" It sounded kind of interesting. I said: "You mean the man with the money is just right out there on the street? Just him and a couple of guards?"

He said: "Well, it ain't all that goddamn easy. I think you ought to take a look at it yourself."

"Well, when do they tote the money over there?"

"That's one of the problems. They ain't no set times. Just whenever they run out. And that depends on how heavy the trading is going."

"How much money you reckon is in the sack?"

He shook his head. "Now that I don't know. But I'd reckon it to be considerable the way money changes hands in that place. Hell, they make trades in the thousands of dollars in a matter of minutes, and that goes on all day."

"Hmmm," I said. "Might be something in it." I leaned back on my elbows on my bed and sat there sipping brandy. Hell, the most exciting thing I'd been thinking about had been Marianne. And now this had come up. Well, that just went to show you. Had been bored for near two weeks and now it was coming all at once.

Wilcey said: "But you need to look it over. You'll probably have to get you a place where you can watch because, like I say, they ain't no set time for it."

I said, curiously, "How come you to know about

this? You sound like you know all about this cotton exchange. You been hanging around down there?"

He ducked his head, acting a little funny about the question. "I been down there a few times," he said.

He was really acting strange. I said, "Doing what? You been planning on going into the cotton business?"

"I've had my reasons," he said, sounding a little defensive about it.

"Wilcey, what the hell have you been up to?"

"Nothing," he said. He got up. "Why don't you take a look at this situation tomorrow? Why don't we go down to the exchange tomorrow and I'll show you what I'm talking about. Go after the noon meal."

He really had my curiosity up now. But I could see he didn't want to talk about it so I let it lay.

In early afternoon we went down to this thing Wilcey called a cotton exchange. It was on the ground floor of one of them big stone-fronted buildings on the main street. We went in through some big double doors, and mainly all I could see was a crowd of men waving pieces of paper in their hands and yelling. It was a big, square room with those marble columns in it, and all these men were gathered up in front of a little thing like a stage. There was a couple of fellows up there in front of a blackboard writing numbers in a bunch of different columns. Seemed like every time they'd write a new number it would cause the crowd to go to screaming and yelling again and waving those little pieces of paper.

We kind of edged around to the side where there were some benches and took a seat. At the back, and on our side, there was a big steel cage with several teller windows in the front of it and a bunch of people inside sitting at desks.

Wilcey nudged me and pointed toward the big steel cage. "Back there is where they got the money. When somebody buys or sells he goes up to one of those windows that says Paying or Receiving and either pays for what he bought or gets paid for what he's sold. I understand they use cash because sometimes some of these people don't want to take drafts or checks so they got to have the money for them."

I asked: "And that cage is where they bring the money to when they bring it here from that bank?"

"Yeah."

I strolled down toward the cage to get a better look. There was both men and women working at the desks, and I could see at least three guards with shotguns in their hands. There must have been a power of money in there for them to have hired so many guards.

I could see right off the bat that we wasn't going to do any business in there. Man would need an army to try and hold up such a place. So I went on back to Wilcey and said, "Well, this is fine. But I want to see what you told me about them transferring money down here from some bank."

I followed him out on the street and then on across to the other side. We walked down about a block and then took up a station where we could see, but not be blocking the sidewalk. We leaned up against a store-front building, standing there smoking. Wilcey gestured across the street. "They come out of that bank down there about a block and then walk the two blocks on down to the Cotton Exchange."

I took note they only crossed one intersection on the way. I said: "Just two guards?"

He looked around at me. "Don't you figure that's enough for this crowded street?"

Of course he was right. The streets were full with people and buggies and wagons.

He said: "And the guy carrying the money is armed too."

We waited about an hour, but nothing happened, so we wandered on back to our hotel. He said: "They don't always need the money every day. Just depends."

I said: "You seem to know hell's own amount about this. Did they have a cotton exchange up there in the Panhandle when you was ranching?"

He said: "Hell no. Are you crazy? They'd only have something like that in a big city."

I said: "Then how come you know so much?"

He looked away. "I told you, I been hanging around down here."

"Well, you're smarter than I give you credit for. I don't reckon I could have figured all that out in such a short time. You ain't been askin' a bunch of questions, have you? Callin' attention to yourself?"

"Hell, Will!" He looked hurt. "I ain't that dumb."

"Just asking."

I thought about Marianne more that night than I did about holding up the Cotton Exchange's money transfer. I didn't know enough about it yet to give much thought time to it.

But I was damned curious as to how Wilcey knew so much. I couldn't, for the life of me, see him going around calling attention to himself by asking a foolish bunch of questions. But other than that I couldn't see how he knew so much. Hell, he hadn't had that much time to watch the thing in operation.

I took me up a place next day not too long after the noon meal. Wilcey had gone off somewhere and I was just as glad. There was some kind of change coming over my old partner, and I wanted some time away from him to try and figure out what was going on with him.

I didn't watch in the morning because Wilcey had told me they never run out of money before afternoon for they always started with plenty. It was generally around mid-afternoon, if the trading was heavy enough, that they needed more cash.

Well, I had plenty of time to cool my heels. I waited around two hours. Fortunately I'd taken my station up in front of a saloon and I could duck in there for a quick beer to relieve the boredom. Finally, just as I was coming out of the saloon, wiping my mouth from having drank a beer too hastily, I saw three men turn out the front of the bank and come marching up the street toward the Cotton Exchange.

Wasn't hard to pick them out. They was walking straight down the sidewalk, three abreast, and all three of them had shotguns in their hands. I watched them until they got to the Cotton Exchange and until they'd disappeared inside. They seemed to know what they was doing and seemed pretty serious about it. For instance, when they got to the door of the exchange, one of the guards had gone inside while the other guard and the man with the money had waited outside. They didn't take the money in until they'd looked and made sure there was no trouble inside. Also, the man carrying the bag had it on a chain with a padlock and the other end chained around his waist. Looked like you'd either have to be able to cut the chain or else take him along with the money.

I walked back to the hotel in a very thoughtful mood. I didn't see a Chinaman's chance of taking that Cotton Exchange money. Wilcey come in around six. I was sitting on my bed smoking and drinking and thinking. We give each other a hello and then he got busy gathering up his shaving gear and a fresh change of clothes. I said: "You going to take another bath tonight?"

He said, "Yeah, pretty hot out there today. I got all sweated up."

I tell you, I didn't even know my old partner anymore.

I sat there doing about what I'd been doing before. He come back in the room looking mighty rushed like he was going off to a meeting with his bankers.

I said: "Where you going, pard?"

"Aw, just out," he said. "Thought I might wander around to some new places tonight."

I said: "I got a look at that money transfer today."

He was busy with his boots. Just like me he'd bought new shop-made boots, and they are sometimes a little hard to get on at first. Though, once you get them on, if you got a good bootmaker, you can't beat them. He stopped with one about half on and looked at me. "Yeah? What'd you think?"

I said: "I think it's damn good you didn't go into the robbing business on your own. Else I don't believe you'd have lived to see the age you're at."

He stared at me. He said: "What the hell's that supposed to mean?"

"It means that if you think that money transfer to the Cotton Exchange is a good prospect for a piece of business, then you been eating loco weed. What did you plan to do with the feller that is chained to the money? Stuff him in your saddlebags along with the gold?"

He said: "Well, I figured you'd know something to do about it."

"And what was you going to do about them three shotguns? Get them to promise not to shoot?"

He didn't say anything.

I said: "And what about the crowd on the streets? About half of which is sheriffs and them uniformed policemen and the rest gents carrying guns in their own rights. What'd you figure to do with them? Ask them in advance to clear the streets and go home early to supper?"

He just sat there looking at me.

I looked back at him, smoking, the smoke from my cigarillo rising in a kind of blue haze between us.

I said: "Now will you tell me what the hell is going on with you?"

He said: "I don't know what you mean."

"Aw, shit!" I was that disgusted. I got up and poured me about a half a water glass full of whiskey, run the rest of it in with water, and then sat back down on my bed. I said: "Goddamn, Wilcey! Don't play the calf with me. And damn sure don't play me for a fool."

He was standing up putting on his gun belt. He said, "Well, I'm blowed if I know what you mean."

"Hell you don't. Here this last week you been taking more baths than any grown man I've ever seen. And shaving! Goddamn, it's a wonder your face ain't wore plumb out. And now you point out a possible job to me."

He was getting a little pink faced. "So what's wrong with that? The job I mean. Hell, you're the one does the figuring. I'd just run up on a situation I thought you might could figure something out about. But if it ain't there, then it ain't there. Hell, pardon me for trying to help."

I almost had to smile. But I said: "There you go, playing me for the fool again. And you was always the levelheaded one in the partnership. Tsk, tsk, tsk."

He faced me. "And what the hell you mean by that?"

I said, "Wilcey, look at it. I know you don't know as much about looking at a job as I do. But I also know you ain't no damn fool. Now, heretofore you been eat alive to get out of this town. All of a sudden you ain't. All of a sudden you're having a damn good time. Then, when you think I might start to be getting a little antsy, that I might not see a chance to do no business around here and we might have to leave,

you sic me on the first thing you see. Just to get me to
spend some time seeing if I can figure out a way to
get our share of their money. Just to keep us around
Houston a little longer. You figured I'd be fool
enough to scratch my brain trying to see what I could
do about robbing that money, knowing that all the
time I'd finally figure out there was no chance. Now
what are you up to!"

He just stared at me.

"Goddamnit, Wilcey! What's going on with you? If
you'd just wanted to stay in Houston awhile that's all
you'd had to tell me. Instead of all these sly tricks
you're trying to play which you ain't worth a damn
at."

Well, he'd got beet red in the face. He said: "It
ain't none of your goddamn business!"

I said, "Hah!"

"Now, damnit!" he said. "Now, damnit!" He pointed
his finger at me. He said: "They'd been plenty of
times you didn't want to talk about something and
you've told me I better leave it alone. And I have.
Well, this is one time I don't want to talk about
something and you *goddamn* well better leave it
alone! You hear me!"

Then he jammed his hat on his head and went
stalking out of the room, slamming the door behind
him.

I was that amazed. Was this my old partner? I'd
never seen the sonofabitch take on so as long as I'd
known him.

Finally I started laughing. Whatever had put a
burr under his saddle had done a damn good job of
it. My first thought, of course, was a woman. But I
knew Wilcey too well to think he'd ever let another
woman get hold of his heart. Lord, when I remembered all the bitter talk and all the lectures he'd
given me. I just couldn't believe it was a woman.

But then I couldn't think of what it could be. Maybe he had run into some politicians and was trying to make himself a respectable life.

In a way it was too bad, for I'd planned on telling him that Marianne was coming and that I'd be taking another room. But he hadn't really seemed in the mood for conversation.

He got in too late that night to talk, and he was alseep when I went down to breakfast so it was the noon meal before I could catch him. Marianne was due the next day and I had determined that if she didn't come, which was what I was about halfway expecting, it would be about time for us to give up on Houston. My plan was for us to head for San Antonio, rendezvous with Chulo, and then set out from there toward whatever I could figure out was the best prospect. Of course, if Marianne did show up, then I was obliged, by my invitation, to stick around for a time. That is, and I couldn't see that, unless she was willing to go on to San Antonio with us.

We pretty much stuck to Delmonico's for the noon meal. We got settled and I said to Wilcey: "Have a good time last night?"

Goddamn if he didn't blush!

But I let it lay. We had enough to talk about without me getting him on the prod. We got our meal ordered and then I said: "Wilcey, I might have to take a room by myself tomorrow. Depending."

"Oh, yeah?" he said.

I said: "Yeah." Hell, he actually looked glad.

He said: "Well, that's just fine. Just let me know. If you like that room the best I could move to another. No trouble."

I just sat there staring at him. I said: "You don't even want to know why? You with more curiosity than an old maid?"

He started to say something, but stopped while the

waiter set our meal of roast beef and potatoes down. When the waiter was gone he said: "Well, why should I be curious? It's your business and you've always had good reasons for everything you did."

I could hardly believe my ears. In the years we'd been running together Wilcey had questioned every decision I'd made, sometimes to the point where I'd practically had to shut him up. And now I was doing something that ought to make him curious as a cat and he was as calm as buttermilk about it, even seemed glad.

I said: "Well, I'm going to tell you anyway. In case you get curious later. I think I've got a woman coming in tomorrow."

"Huh?" He was about to take a bite and he looked up over his fork. "A woman? Where from?"

"Galveston," I said.

He said: "When'd you get a chance to meet any women in Galveston. Hell, we were barely there two days."

"The whore," I said, "that I was with that first night."

He stared at me. "A whore? You mean you're importing a whore? My God, Wilson, they ain't no shortage of whores in this town."

I said: "This one is different."

He commenced to looking agitated. "Listen, you can't do that."

"I can't? Why not?"

"You just can't. Hell, have you lost your mind? What the hell you want to bring a whore here for? You ain't thinking of moving her into that hotel, are you?"

I kind of reared back and looked at him. He was getting mighty excited. A minute ago he'd been telling me that what I was doing was none of his business. And now here he was trying to protect the best interests of some hotel. I pointed this out to him and then added, "Besides, who's going to know she's a whore? You going to go around telling people?"

He was getting more and more agitated. He said: "Oh, hell, you can't hide a thing like that! Goddamn, people can spot a whore a mile off. Especially another woman!"

I said, "How'd a woman get into this? I thought it was the hotel you was worrying about."

"Just never mind that, just never mind that. Listen, Will, you can't do this. You can't bring no whore here to Houston. Go see her in Galveston, but don't bring her here to the same hotel me and you is at."

I was looking at him in amazement. I said: "I didn't hear you right. I know I didn't. I know you didn't just say I couldn't bring her to Houston."

"Well—" He opened his mouth and then closed it. Then he said, "Maybe I put that wrong."

I said dryly, "Maybe you did."

"All right." He kind of leaned forward. "All right, how about as a favor to me."

I put my fork down. "I swear," I said, "I believe you have taken leave of your senses. Since when did it become any of your business what I do about women?"

"But a whore!"

"What is this? What have you done? Joined the Baptist church? What do you care if she's a whore or a circus acrobat? You act like you've never seen one before."

He said, "Look, as a favor to me."

I shook my head. "I don't know what's going on with you. You been acting as strange as any man I've ever seen. Now you want me to do you this favor, you're going to have to tell me why and you're going to have to have a damn good reason."

He looked away. "I ain't ready to tell you yet."

"Why not? You done something awful? I know, I bet you've joined the Women's Christian Temperance Union and you're going to get me to stop drinking."

"Now don't joke around, Will. This is serious. Listen, I'll tell you in a couple of days."

"She'll be here tomorrow," I reminded him. "Or I hope she will be."

He said: "If I tell you you'll laugh at me, and I don't want you to laugh at me. Not about this."

"How do you know I'll laugh?" Hell, I was about half enjoying myself. I'd never seen him so agitated. And all that hoorahing he'd give me over the years, all the horse laughs he'd give me? Hell, I didn't know what he was going to tell me, but I was damn well going to laugh, whether it was funny or not. I said: "I won't laugh, Wilcey. I promise."

"You promise?" He was looking at me hard. "You'll treat it as serious as it is? You won't make sport of something that means a lot to me?"

"I promise," I lied.

He looked away. Finally he said: "Well, there's this woman." Then he looked at me quickly to see my reaction.

I kept my face straight. "What woman?"

"Well, it's this lady I've met." He drug in a deep breath. "I'm kind of taken with her."

"Oh, yeah? Hell, that sounds wonderful, Wilcey. Tell me about her. Where'd you meet her?"

He looked down and said, "Well, she works down there at the Cotton Exchange. She's one of them in that cage back there that keeps the books."

"Oh, ho!" I said. Now it was all starting to make sense. No wonder he knew so much about the place. She'd been telling him. "You just walk in there and meet her?"

"Well, no," he said. "Not exactly. I wandered in there one day and saw her back there. I don't know, I just kept going back. Then one day she went in that little café next door and I followed her in there and just up and asked if I could eat with her." His face lit up. "She let me. And we just got along like all get out. After that she let me take her out to dinner."

Boy, he was smitten. You could see it all over his face. I started to laugh. He looked at me, outraged, his face going beet red. "Goddamn you!" he said. "You promised you wouldn't laugh!"

I tried to choke it down. He really was serious. I said, "I can't help it. You ought to of seen your face while you was talking about her."

"You quit laughing!" Boy, he was mad as a wet settin' hen.

I gradually got hold of myself. He reminded me of a reformed drunk. You know them kind that are the worst about spouting about the evils of drink. Then they finally break down and take one and they can get drunker faster than the steadiest drinker around.

That was Wilcey. All I'd heard from him was that they wasn't no good women. But now he'd been hit.

I said: "Well, tell me more about her."

He was still mad for me laughing. But now that he was started, he wanted to talk about this woman. He said: "Well, she's a real lady. She's a widder woman. Got two little kids."

"How old is she?"

"Why, I never asked. About thirty, I'd guess."

"Where's she live?"

"Out of downtown just a little. Four or five blocks from the Exchange. She's got a little house there. Her husband was with the railroad. He died of consumption or some such. She's having a hard time of it, what with her two children, but you'd never know it to hear her. She don't complain about nothing!"

"Then how do you know she's having a hard time of it?"

"Huh? Well, hell! I ain't dumb. Just little things she lets drop. But she didn't even know she was giving anything away. She's got too much pride."

"Oh, no," I said dryly. "Of course not."

"Now what do you mean by that?" He was starting to get angry again. Boy, he was touchy about that woman.

"Nothing," I said, "nothing." But I did look at him over a cigarillo and kind of smiled. "So that's where you been sleeping them nights you didn't come home."

Boy, I thought he'd blushed before, but it wasn't nothing to the color his face went then. He said, "Now goddamn, you keep your mouth off that! You hear me? You let that alone."

I wanted to ask him what the kids thought about mama having a man sleep over, but I thought I'd better not. Likely they were used to it. But I did ask, trying to sound as innocent as I could, "What do the children call you? Uncle Dennis?"

"Huh?" It taken him aback for a minute. Then he said, "Why yes, as a matter of fact they do. What the hell difference does that make?"

I just smiled some more, picturing mama carefully tutoring the kids to call Wilcey Uncle. Likely it wasn't their first lesson. I said, "Well, have you managed to overcome her pride enough to get her to let you lend her some money?"

He didn't much want to answer. But he finally said, "Well, yeah, now that you mention it. But it wasn't much. Few hundred dollars." Then he said, "But I damn near had to fight her to make her take it. And she wasn't even going to tell me about it. I had to worm it out of her."

"Oh, yeah? How'd you manage that?"

"Well," he said, "a few days ago I wanted to hire a buggy and for us to take a drive in the country

directly she got off work. But she couldn't, she had to
go to the bank. Well, I couldn't see where that'd take
all that much time, but she said it was serious and
would take all kinds of time. We were having supper
together and, Will, that brave little lady just broke
down and started crying. The bank was about to take
her house away from her, and she was going in and
try and get them to delay just one more month! And,
by God, she hadn't mentioned one word to me before.
Not until I wanted her to take that buggy ride! Now
that ought to prove something. If she'd been wanting
money off me, she'd of damn well brought it up before. But, no, it was only to make me understand that
it took a real serious matter to keep her from going
buggy riding with me. That's the only reason she finally give in and told me."

"I bet you couldn't get the money to her fast
enough, could you?"

"Listen," he said, with a little heat in his voice,
"Dennis Wilcey ain't ever been slow when it comes to
helping his friends. You ought to know that."

I just sat there marveling at him. I couldn't believe
it was the same man I'd been closer than a brother
with. Boy, that woman had fried his brains. I tell you
I believe a woman can addle a man faster than liquor
can. Hell, I'd seen Wilcey so drunk he couldn't hit
the ground with his hat and he'd never acted as
dumb as he was now.

But I knew there was no point in saying anything
to him. And, God knows, I'd of been the last one to
call the pot black. Because, for sheer addle brainness,
I believed I'd been the champeen of all time where
women was concerned.

I said: "But I still don't see where this has ought to
do with me, me and my whore."

He looked astonished. "Why, of course it does. I've
talked to her about you. Told her you and me had

been partners for a long time. She can't wait to meet
you, and, as a matter of fact, I was going to arrange
for us all to have dinner tomorrow night so ya'll
could get to know one another." He give me a kind
of shit-eatin' grin. "You might have to stand up as my
best man before long."

I said, "Partner—" Then I stopped. He was going
to have to find out for himself. So I said: "So? So
we're all going to get to be old buddies. What does
that have to do with Marianne coming here?"

"Well, goddamn, Will! She knows you and I are
partners. Sooner or later she'll see you with that
whore and she'll know she's a whore. Then what'll
that make her think of you? Running around town
with a two-bit whore. And whatever she thinks of you
is going to be what she thinks of me. Goddamn, Ruth
is a lady! Maybe the first one I ever met."

I said: "What does she think you do, Wilcey?"

He looked down. "Well, I told her I was a cattle
buyer. Like I've heard you say."

"You figure she won't find out you're an outlaw?
Sooner or later? What happens after you get married
and are all settled down in your little love nest and
the sheriff comes around? What do you think she'll
think then?"

He looked a little miserable. "I ain't worrying
about that right now."

"And how are you going to make a living? You
ain't got enough of a stake to get back into ranching.
You ain't even got enough of a stake to go back to
gambling, not big-time gambling."

He said, "Listen, here's what I thought. If we could
pull off just one more job, just make one more big
payday, why then I'd have money enough to buy me
a ranch somewhere and go straight honest. She'd never
find out."

I almost laughed out loud it sounded so familiar.

Just one more job, just one more big payday and
then be an honest man forever. God, for how many
years had I sung that old song? And how many last
jobs did I pull? Hell, as late as a year ago I was still
handing myself that line. I said, "Wilcey, how many
times you heard me say that?"

He looked down at his plate. He damn near hadn't
eaten a bite. He said, "I know. But with me it's different. You was always a bandit." He looked up and suddenly banged his fist so hard on the table that a
couple of waiters looked our way. He said: "But goddamnit! It's different with me. I *was* a rancher! I can
do it again." He sat back in his chair, looking at me,
his eyes kind of wild.

I swear, I felt sorry for him. Unfortunately, I knew
how he felt.

He said: "So will you head that whore off? Help
me make it look like you and me is respectable
businessmen?"

I shook my head. "No."

It took him a moment. He said, "What?"

I told him again. "No, I won't."

"Goddamn, Will, I'm asking you a favor."

"No, you're not. Something like that isn't a favor.
It's too damn much more than that. Besides, if she
doesn't come I'm pulling up stakes and heading for
San Antonio."

He got agitated again. "Will, you got to do this.
I've already pointed you out on the street to her. We
were sitting by a window in a café and you come by.
If she don't think you're respectable, she won't think
I am."

It hurt me, but I said, "I ain't going to do it, Dennis. Now get that straight in your head. If Marianne
comes I'm going to move her into the hotel with me
and keep her here as long as she'll stay. Goddamnit,
I'm lonely too!"

He said, "But a whore!"

I said, "Listen—" My voice got harsh. I leaned across the table at him. I said, "Listen, maybe a whore is all I can get. But at least she's an honest whore."

"What do you mean by that?"

"Whatever you think I mean."

"And you ain't going to do me this favor?"

"No. I done told you. No."

He got up. "Then me and you ain't partners no more." And goddamn if he didn't jam his hat on his head and go stalking out of the restaurant.

Chapter Five

~~~~~~

Next morning Wilcey came into the room before I was out of bed. I don't know where he'd spent the night, probably at his girlfriend's house. He sat down on his bunk and unplugged the brandy and poured himself out a little and added some water. He held the bottle up to me. "Want some?"

I shook my head. I'd got pretty drunk the night before and my mouth tasted like raw dog with no salt. I swung my legs around, reached over and got the water pitcher, swished a mouthful around, and then spit it on the floor. Then I lit a cigarillo. I didn't say anything, just sat there looking at Wilcey, waiting to see if he'd come to make another damn fool out of himself.

He cleared his throat a couple of times and then finally said, "I don't know what got into me yesterday, acting like that."

"I do," I said. "You're in love." Hell, I wasn't going to make it easy on him.

He pinked up a little at that, but didn't say nothing for a moment. Finally he kind of sighed. "Maybe you're right. Maybe I ain't thinking so damn good right now."

I didn't say anything, figuring my silence was

enough assent and there wasn't any use rubbing it in.

Finally he looked over at me. "I guess it wouldn't do me any good to ask you to just kind of keep her out of sight."

I shook my head.

He sighed. "Well, I hope you didn't pay much attention to what I said yesterday."

I said: "Well, I don't know, Wilcey. Ain't no law says you got to partner up with me."

"Oh, goddamn, Wilson, don't make it so damn hard on me. I was wrong. I'm admitting it. But, goddamn, you've made a fool out of yourself over a woman before. I seem to distinctly remember after we robbed that poker game and we had to knock you out and tie you to a chair to keep you from going back into El Paso to find her. And I remember you had to go in and meet that woman in Amarillo and damn near got yourself killed. And I ain't even going to mention that little senorita in Sabinas Hidalgo that you panted after for all the years I've known you."

Well, I had to remain silent for he had me dead to rights. Only thing I could have said was that I wasn't *still* making a fool out of myself over them as he was. But I just said: "Aw, hell, forget it."

He said: "I told Ruth last night that you and I had had a disagreement and she was awful upset about it."

I said: "You did what!"

He said hastily, "Oh, I didn't tell her what about. I just said we'd had a disagreement about business, and she thought I ought to try and work it out with you. Wilson, she's an awful good woman. I wish you'd come and meet her."

"I will," I said.

He poured himself some more cognac. "Will, you know what she told me last night? She said there was near fifty thousand dollars in most of those pouches they deliver from the bank. Fifty thousand dollars! Goddamn, split three ways that'd give me better than fifteen thousand dollars, and that with what I already got would give me more than enough to buy a good ranch and stock it. Will, ain't there some way you can figure where we can rob that situation?"

I thought a minute, smoking. Finally I poured myself a little cognac and water and took a few sips. Then I said: "Wilcey, think real hard. Think back to when you first met Ruth. Did you ask about them pouches, that money transfer? Or did she pop out with it? I mean, how'd it come to be brought up in the first place."

He looked startled. "Well, I don't know. I never thought about it."

"How could it have been you if you didn't know anything about it in the first place?"

He scratched his head. "Weeell, I guess it couldn't have been me. I guess Ruth got to talking about all the money they handle and I guess I got interested and started asking some questions. I guess maybe she brought it up. Why?"

But I said: "Do you really believe Ruth thinks you're a cattle buyer?"

"Of course. Why shouldn't she? That's what I told her."

I said: "Shit!" and flipped my cigarillo out the open window. "Hell, Wilcey, you don't even look like a cattle buyer no more. Maybe four years ago you could have passed for one, but not now. Look at that cut-down holster you wear. Look at the way you got your gun rig set up. Look at the way you carry yourself. Look at how hard your face has got. Wilcey, we both look like what we are. She don't believe you're a cattle buyer. She *knows* what you are."

"Aw, shit, Will. That's a gentle woman. Until her

husband died I bet she wasn't out of the house half a dozen times. She don't know what a cattle buyer looks like. And she damn sure don't know what a outlaw looks like. And what are you gettin' at anyway?"

"Nothing," I said. "Nothing. Let it go." I got up and commenced putting on my clothes. I figured it was about time to go shave and have a bath and get ready to go meet that train. Though I figured it was just going to be a waste of time. As I started out the door to the bathroom I said: "Don't worry. We're all square. I'll figure out something."

He was gone from the room when I got back from shaving and taking a bath. I dressed carefully, though I didn't know what for. She wasn't going to be there anyway.

But I spent a little time thinking about Wilcey's lady friend, and mighty interesting she was too. Main thing I was interested in was why she was feeding a cattle buyer so much information about money that was out on the street. Well, if anybody was going to find out what that lady was up to, I reckoned it was going to have to be me. It was plenty obvious that Wilcey was so blinded by love he couldn't tell his ass from a horseshoe. But if he thought he was going to talk me into a robbery on that money transfer just so he could get enough money to win his lady love, he had another think coming.

I finally left to go down to the train depot. Damn, I was nervous. I had to stop in a couple of bars on the way down to get a drink, just to get myself somewhat calmed down. And if that ain't a pretty comedown for a man like me I don't know what was. Didn't seem as if I'd ever been this nervous over meeting a woman, especially a woman I'd only known for a few days.

I got to the train depot about fifteen minutes early, and it was crowded with outgoing passengers. Hell, I thought, even if she comes I'll never be able to find her in such a mob.

I walked outside and smoked a cigarillo, pacing around impatiently, and cussing myself for even caring whether or not she came. Finally, way off down the tracks I heard the sound of a steam engine, and then I heard him blowing for the crossings just outside of town. I hurried around to the front of the station and joined the bunch that was crowding the loading platform. The train come around a bend and then straightened up for the run into the station. Finally, it braked to a stop in front of the loading platform, blowing steam and making all kinds of noises. The porters come out of the chair cars and set their little stools down under the steps the passengers unloaded down. There were six chair cars and I got myself stationed right in the middle of the bunch, figuring to be able to see her in either direction. I also figured that if she was on the train, she'd be the last one out so I'd have more time to sweat.

Which is about the way my luck runs.

But I'll be damned if she wasn't the first one off the car that was right in front of me. She come down the steps wearing some kind of frilly, ankle-length white gown and a little white hat and, damn, she looked pretty. The porter was right behind her setting her bag on the ground. She thanked him and I seen her give him a dollar.

So she'd brought a bag. Well, maybe she wasn't joshing me. Maybe she intended to stay a few days. She stood there on the platform, looking around, the crowd milling by her as they rushed to board the cars. I stepped forward, sweeping off my hat as I did. I said: "Pardon, ma'am, but I'm Mister Jim Wilson's man and he sent me to fetch you."

She give me a slow smile, it just kind of gradually

worked its way through her soft face. She said: "Here I am. Surprised?"

"Not at all," I lied. "Are you?"

She shook her head. "Naw. You looked to me like a man knew a good thing when he seen it."

"You too," I said.

I picked up her bag in my left hand and she put her hand through my arm and we strolled off that loading platform just as big as you please. You'd of thought I was the king pin of the county and she was the visiting crème de la crème.

We didn't say anything for about a block, and then she wanted to know where we were staying. I told her the Texas Hotel and she give me a look.

"Kind of a high-toned place. You sure they'll let me in there?"

I said, "Well, you don't suck your teeth after you eat, do you? And you won't shoot up the bar?"

She said: "I'm serious."

I stopped and set the suitcase down and faced her. I said: "Do you expect them to know you here?"

She shook her head. "No, but desk clerks can spot my kind a mile away."

I said: "Look here, let's get something straight. You know what I am and I know what you are. And if it don't bother either one of us, which are the interested parties, then we don't give a damn what anyone else thinks. If trouble comes we'll handle it then, until then let's don't get a burr under our saddle blanket about it."

She looked at me a long moment. "You know, whatever your name is, you're a hell of a fellow."

It kind of embarrassed me. I said, "What the hell," and picked up her bag and we started on toward the hotel.

I had kind of anticipated the problem. The day before I'd taken another room and I had the key in my pocket. It had kind of mystified the desk clerk, because he knew I already had a room. I'd said: "My partner snores. I got to be able to get some sleep."

So when we got to the hotel, we just swept on up the stairs to our room as pretty as you please and no one the wiser. At the right number I unlocked and flung the door back and she went on in.

She said: "This is nice."

And it was. It was a corner room with windows on two walls and nice wallpaper and a big, oversized double bed. There was also a nightstand and a desk and a couple of chairs.

I said: "Hell it ought to be nice. Costing me five dollars a day."

She turned around to me and smiled. She said: "The hell it is! My God, am I worth it?"

I knew she'd take a drink so I had a bottle of cognac sitting on the table, and I poured us out one and raised my glass to her. I said, "Luck," and she done likewise. I watched to see if she'd knock hers all the way back as befits the toast and damned if she didn't do it. There's damn few women know to do that.

"Pretty good French cognac," she said.

I poured us out another round. She sat down on the bed and I sat down in one of the chairs and just kind of looked at her. Damn she looked pretty and I didn't see how any desk clerk in the country could pick her out for a whore.

I said: "There's a bathroom on each floor. One down here at the end of the hall. Got plenty of hot water if you want to take a bath."

"Lord," she said, "I'd love a bath. I wanted to get one this morning, but we were so busy last night that all the girls were in there this morning and I had to take a little sitz bath in my room. And that's not much comfort."

It kind of stabbed my heart when she said how busy they were last night. I had no business letting it hurt me for I knew what she was. But I still said, "Well, maybe being so busy was worth it. Maybe you made a lot of money."

She heard the tone in my voice and she give me a look. She said evenly, "That kind of talk ain't going to help either one of us, cowboy. You said you knew what we both were."

I looked away from her. "All right. I was wrong." I hesitated a second, trying to understand why it'd caused that quick pain in my heart when she'd said that about the night before. I said slowly, "I wasn't thinking for a second. I was acting like a damn schoolboy. But you looked so damn pretty sitting there in your white dress and your little white hat that, for a second, I almost felt like I was taking the town belle to the May dance."

Then it was her turn to be silent. Finally she got up and walked over to me. First she put her hand on the top of my head, then she cupped it behind my neck and softly drew my face into the softness of her belly. She said, with just the same touch of sadness in her voice that I was feeling, she said, "I know, darlin'. I never got to go to the May dance neither."

I put my arms around her and hugged her to my face. Then, after a moment, I pushed her away. I said, kind of gruffly, for I was worried about what I was going to ask, "Get on back, woman. Go sit on the bed. I still got something I want to get settled."

She went back and sat on the bed. I took a sip of my brandy and then looked over at her. I started to speak then stopped and took another drink of brandy.

She said: "What the hell is it, for God's sake?"

I said, a little gruffly, for I didn't know how to put in other than to come out and say it, I said, "Listen, are you expecting me to pay you while you're here with me?"

She kind of half turned her head and looked at me for a long moment. Then she said, softly, "No, darlin', I ain't expectin' you to pay me. Your telegram asked me if I wanted a vacation." Then she suddenly smiled. "But I do expect you to show me a damn good time."

I was embarrassed. I said, "Marianne, I know how bad that sounded for me to ask you, but I—"

She said, "I understand, darlin'. I understand why you asked it. Don't worry."

I still felt a little bad about it. I said: "I wanted to get it straight between us. I wanted to know for sure why you came."

She said, smiling, "I came because I wanted to, cowboy. And for no other reason."

I stood up and went over and kissed her on the mouth. She tried to lean back and pull me over on her, but I resisted. I said, "Not just yet, my fat baby. You go take your bath and then we'll see how it goes."

I went back and sat down in my chair, sipping at my brandy. She looked at me and shook her head. "God, you're a good-looking man. Maybe I ought to ask if you're going to charge me."

I said, "Go take your bath."

The truth was I wanted the touch of them other men off her before I took her to bed. But I wasn't going to say that because it wasn't right for me to feel that way.

She gathered up a change of clothes out of her suitcase and I showed her where the bathroom was. Then I went back and sat down to await her return. I was in a high state of excitement.

She come back in a robe. It wasn't that flimsy lavender robe she'd had on that afternoon in the

whorehouse, but a good substanial robe that a lady
might wear down a hotel hallway coming back from
her bath. When she come in the room and I saw her,
I damn well wished Wilcey could have been there to
see her and maybe then he wouldn't have been so
damn fast in his condemnation.

I'd taken off my boots, but nothing else, and I was
sitting there in a chair, drinking cognac and wiggling
my bare toes. She just give me a wink when she come
in the door and then went to the closet and hung up
the clothes she'd worn down to the bathhouse.

When she was through with her clothes, she come
over and gathered my head up in her arms and
hugged me to her. Her robe had parted and my cheek
was against her bare belly. I said, "Oh, hell, Marianne, I'm so damn glad to see you."

From above me she said, "I know, cowboy. I feel
the same way. Damn you."

I said, "What do you mean by that?"

"I mean, you're complicating my life. It was all
pretty well set. Until you come along. Hell, I ain't got
no business being in Houston."

Then I knew what she meant, for I felt the same
way. I said, "Listen, don't get me all hot and bothered
right now. I, for some reason, want to take this kind
of slow. Why don't we lay down and take a nap, nothing more, and then go out and eat a hell of a supper
and then come back here?"

She said: "Oh, you beautiful man!"

She pulled away from me and looked down and
smiled into my face. Then she took my face in both
of her hands and leaned down and kissed me gently
on the lips. She said, "Oh, what a relaxation you
are."

I said, "I want to talk to you, Marianne. Right now
that's what I want to do more than anything else."

She just hugged me, she didn't say nothing else.

So we laid down in bed together. We didn't have any clothes on, but it wasn't nothing that had to do with fucking. We were just laying there, holding on to each other. I reckon that made me some kind of softy, but I didn't care. I just lay there, letting a good deal of the hurt run out of me, through my old rough skin, just laying there holding her soft body next to mine.

I guess I felt like an old bear laid up in his den, licking his wounds, getting ready to go back out and take on whatever might come along. I didn't care what the reason was. All I knew was that it felt damn good. Hell, I was tired of being so damn tough. Just damn tired of it.

After a while we went to sleep. I don't know how long we slept, but when I awoke, twilight was outside the window.

I got the water pitcher and took me a drink and swished it around in my mouth and spit it on the floor. Marianne had been sleeping up against me, sleeping quietly, but the noise roused her and she began to stir. She sat up. For a minute all she did was stretch. I looked at her, seeing her fine breasts hanging down where the sheet had fallen off them. Then, almost without looking, she suddenly turned and flung her arms around me. "Oh, love," she said, "I feel so good. Hug me."

Well, I did. But I would have anyway without any prompting.

I let her go and swung my legs over the side of the bed and lit a cigarillo and poured us each out a glass of brandy and water. She sat up beside me, just kind of leaning over against my back.

I handed her a glass over my shoulder and she took it and sipped contentedly. "Ah," she said, "that tastes good."

We sat there in contentment and then she began

rubbing her hand over my back. "God," she said, "you've got the broadest back of any man." Then she laid her cheek up against it.

I said, "Of all the men?"

Which was the wrong thing to say. She jerked away. "Listen," she said, a little heat in her tone, "let's get it straight. I don't put my hands, much less my cheek, on that many men's backs. And if I tell you that I mean it."

I'd made another mistake. I said: "All right."

She said: "I guess I'm your first woman. I guess you never been in bed with another woman."

I said: "Look, let it go."

I'd ruined a damn good moment. But that was me for you. I never could let well enough alone.

She kind of pulled away from me and then wouldn't say anything. For a long, miserable minute I just sat there. Then I turned around to her. I said: "Listen, I ain't used to a woman being sweet to me. I guess there just ain't a lot of trust in my soul." I said it into her breasts, not looking at her. Then I looked up into her face. "Listen, I been as nervous as a schoolboy about you coming here to me. I don't know why, little time as you and I've known each other. But there it is. You want to take advantage of it, go right ahead. I'm laying myself open to being suckered. But you'll only do it once."

Then I turned back around, my face kind of hot. A man didn't tell a woman such things. And why I was telling Marianne was more than I could reason out.

She was silent for a moment, and then she put her hand on my back again. She said: "Who the hell are you?"

I looked around at her. I didn't mind telling her with no fear of her turning me in. But I was a little worried that she might recognize the name and be horrified. I've heard some stories about myself that not only weren't true, but didn't really present me at my best. I don't mind the exaggerations about the robberies I've done, but I don't like it when they make me out a bloodthirsty killer. I said to her: "How long you been in Texas?"

She said, "Oh, about five years."

"Ain't spent any time on the border, have you?"

"Just El Paso. I guess San Antonio don't count. Why?"

"I don't know," I said.

"Well?" she said after a moment.

"Well what?"

"Who the hell are you? You told me you wanted to talk."

"Why do you want to know?"

"Because."

"Because why?"

"Just because. Goddamnit, I want to know about *you*. Do I have to spell it out? And a name, your real name is a good place to start. I already know you're an outlaw. What the hell else you got to hide after that?"

I lit a cigarillo. When it was drawing good I said, "My name is Wilson Young."

I was looking away from her so I didn't see the reaction on her face. For a minute I thought she was going to say, "So what?" but then I felt a movement behind me. I looked around. She'd jumped down to the end of the bed and was kneeling, looking at me. She said, "Wilson Young! Are you really Wilson Young?"

Her eyes were wide, her face excited. I said, "I think I am. At least that's what my mama and daddy told me."

"My God," she said. "You're a *famous* outlaw!"

I said, "Well, that's kind of a mixed blessing. If

you're going to be an outlaw, it's generally for the best not to be famous."

"But I've heard of you. I've heard stories about you! Once in the house I was working in in El Paso a guy come in and tried to pass himself off as you. You'd robbed a poker game there or something. When they found out it wasn't really you, they beat the shit out of him. But until then he had everybody scared half to death. My God, you're supposed to be mean and tough and a killer. You don't seem mean and tough to me."

"I didn't to my mother either." I poured out some more brandy and water. "Look," I said, "can we let this alone for a while? Why don't you get dressed and we'll go out and get a bite to eat."

"I can't get over it," she said. "I just can't get over it. My God, I'm in the same room, the same bed with an honest to God outlaw! Me, Marianne Mason from Tulsa, Oklahoma."

I said, "Will you shut up and get dressed!"

Finally, she got out of bed and began putting on her clothes. I moved over to a chair where I could watch her, enjoying it. That's about as good as it gets, sitting, drinking and smoking, and watching a damn good-looking woman get dressed. Only thing better than that is smoking and drinking and watching a damn good-looking woman get undressed.

When she was ready I started laughing. She was wearing a very trim, very proper blue dress that buttoned all the way up to her throat.

She said: "What's so funny?"

"Nothing," I said. "I just wish Wilcey was here."

"Who's Wilcey?"

"He's my partner," I said. I told her a little about Wilcey and his girlfriend and his fear of me having a whore come to town. Then I said, "If he could see you now, he'd probably think I'd kidnapped the banker's daughter."

She said, "You don't think I look like a whore?"

"Hell no!" I said. "But then I never thought you looked like a whore. Even in a red velvet dress."

I had my clothes on by then and we went on downstairs and started for Delmonico's. I was very conscious, as we walked along, of all the looks she got from the men we passed. Made me feel pretty damn good.

I said: "How long you been a working girl?"

She had her hand in my arm. "Oh, I don't know. I was eighteen when I started. I'm twenty-five now. Seven years then."

"You like it?"

She shrugged and pulled a face. "It sure as hell beats the kind of work I was doing on my daddy's farm. But then anything would have beat that."

"But you had other selections," I said. "You could have got married. I bet every beaux in the county was bidding for your hand."

"Sure I could have," she said. "But I'd just been trading one farm for another. The work would have been the same. I had my mother to go by. When I left she was thirty-six and looked sixty. I vowed that wasn't going to happen to me. The only time she had any rest was when she was about to deliver another kid. But that only lasted a week. My father couldn't believe that being pregnant was any excuse not to work in the fields."

"How'd you get away? Run off?"

"Naw. Classic story. Run off with a lightning rod drummer. Second night out he got drunk in the hotel in Oklahoma City, and I rolled him for his poke and set out on my own. Run in to some girls that worked in a saloon in Dallas and they got me set up. Been on my own ever since."

We got to the door of Delmonico's and went on in. Well, we was both pretty hungry so we just up and ordered a dozen raw oysters apiece just to get started. Then Marianne wanted to know if I'd ever had oysters with champagne. Hell, I'd never even had champagne.

She said, "It costs a lot. Have you got plenty of money?"

"Hell, yes," I said. "Let's get us some of that champagne."

Well, they brought it, and though I wouldn't want to have it as a regular thing, it went down well with the oysters. We had about three glasses of that bubbly wine while we were eating the oysters, and I swear, it was starting to make me a little high. Of course, I'd had considerable brandy beforehand, but I can generally drink pretty steady without getting drunk. And Marianne was doing a pretty good amount of giggling herself. She said: "The hell with anything else. Let's just eat oysters and drink champagne. You know what they say about oysters."

"No, what?"

She held a limp finger out and then all of a sudden made it go stiff. Then she looked at me and laughed.

It took me a minute to get it, and I asked her if she was sure. She said, "That's what they say."

I turned and yelled for the waiter. "Bring us some more oysters and keep them coming."

Well, we stayed about two hours, eating oysters and drinking champagne. I reckon we downed about four bottles of that stuff, and when we left, I was tight as a tick and Marianne was laughing at everything I said.

We got back to the door of the hotel and I said, in a whisper, "Now, we don't want to attract no attention. You got to keep a straight face while we walk across this here lobby."

Well, that just struck her as the funniest thing

she'd ever heard, and I had to get her plumb away from the door of the hotel until she got over her fit.

Finally, we kind of set our faces and sailed through the door and across the lobby to the stairs. I rushed her the last few feet because I could see from the way she was getting red in the face that she was about to bust. Luckily we were about halfway up the stairs and out of sight of the lobby before the dam broke. Then she just laughed until she got so weak she couldn't climb the stairs.

When she finally wound down, I kissed her, standing there on the stairs, and that seemed to take all the giggles out of her. She kissed me back, hard. Then she whispered in my ear, "Let's hurry."

We went to the room and I undressed and got in bed and then lay there, watching her, while she put me on a little show of getting out of her clothes. Then she was climbing in bed with me, putting her soft, smooth body next to mine. I had intended that we should make slow, sweet love, make it last for a long, long time. It started off that way, but then she got on top of me and put me inside of her and it was all over in an instant.

She laughed a little, but not much. I think she was as disappointed as I was. Maybe more. I said: "Goddamn them oysters!"

So for a little while we just laid there next to each other, on our backs, holding hands and staring up at the ceiling. Finally I reached over and lit a cigarillo and lay there smoking. I didn't want anything else to drink. That champagne was still buzzing in my head.

She said: "What are you doing in Houston?"

I said, "Nothing. Just seemed like a good place to rest up a little. I kinda hoped we might find some business to do, there being so much money in the place. But I can't get a line on nothing reasonable."

She said: "You don't have a job planned here?" She sounded almost disappointed.

I said: "No, and even if I did I wouldn't tell you."

She didn't say anything to that. I didn't expect it to hurt her. She'd been around enough—she knew men in my profession didn't talk about their business that much.

I said: "It just seems like a good place to hole up. I'm way off my range, which is the border country, and nobody, so far, has recognized me. It's mighty nice for a change."

Then I looked over at her. We had the gaslight on and I could see her profile clearly. I said: "And how about you? How long before you have to go back to Galveston?"

She said: "I'm not going back to Galveston. I quit that house. I got everything I need for the time being in that suitcase and my trunk is packed back in Galveston. All they're waiting for is instructions as to where to ship it."

I raised up on my elbows and looked at her. I said, "Can you just quit like that?"

She said, "Hell, yes. Those people don't own me. They didn't really think a high-class whore like me was going to stay around very long anyway. I'm tired of having them damn foreign sailors pawing over me and trying to beat me down on my price. They ain't got the money for a woman like me."

She was like that. Sometimes she could sound so sweet and innocent and other times she could sound as hard as a crosscut saw.

I said: "Well, how long you planning on taking a vacation? I mean, staying here with me?"

She turned her face and gave me that slow, sweet smile. "As long as I want to, cowboy." Then she laughed. "If you got the money, sweetheart, I got the time."

"You got no plans?"

She said: "Oh, I been thinking of going north. Maybe to Chicago. I hear they pay big money up there. And I've never seen that part of the country." She turned her face to me. "You know, I ain't got that many more years to hang on to the looks. One of these days I'll be on the down side of the hill. I've seen some of them whores up in their thirties and still trying to hang on. Their price getting lower and lower until they'll almost fuck for a drink and a meal." Her face got hard. "Well, that ain't going to happen to me. Just like I wouldn't let what happened to my mama happen to me. So I'm going where the money is, make my pile, and get out while the getting's good."

I got out of bed and walked over to the window and looked out. I had to say that I knew how she felt. My mind turned back a number of years to when me and Les and Tod Richter and Harlan Thomas and his partner Chico was setting up to rob the bank in Uvalde. An old, wore-out gunman named Kid Blanco had followed Tod out from town and wanted in on the job. He was finished, through. And yet he was still trying to hang on, hang on when his nerve was gone, his speed was gone, his brains were gone. He'd tried to impress me by picking a fight with Tod. Then Harlan Thomas had killed him just as nonchalantly as you'd kill a bug, and Harlan was a long way from a top hand. At the time it had happened I'd made me a vow that I was never going to end up like a Kid Blanco. When I was through, I was going to be through. I wasn't going to be no gray-haired old ex-gunfighter hanging on and whining to be taken on just one more job. Her words had disturbed me.

From the bed she said: "What's the matter?"

"Nothing," I said. I left the window and went back to the bed and lit a cigarillo. Only I didn't lay down, just sat on the edge, thinking. After a moment she put her hand on my thigh.

"What's the matter, Wilson?"

"I said, nothing."

She was quiet a moment and then she said, "You didn't like me talking about Chicago, did you?"

I didn't say anything.

"You didn't like me talking about making my pile. You don't like me talking about my business, do you?"

I still didn't say anything.

She said: "Wilson, you really don't like it because I'm a whore. Do you?"

I said: "Hell, Marianne, you were a whore when I met you. I ain't got any right to think otherwise."

She said: "But now it's got different, hasn't it?"

I drew on my cigarillo. Finally, I said: "Yeah, kinda."

She said: "I know. I feel it too."

I quickly said: "Let's don't talk about it anymore."

"All right."

I turned off the gaslight and we lay very close together. After a time I said: "In other words, if you ain't going back to Galveston, and I don't want to stay in Houston, you'd be willing to go somewhere with me?"

She pulled herself a little closer. "As long as it's this good I'd go goddamn near anywhere with you."

I said: "Maybe we'll go up north. I know they wouldn't be looking for me there, and I need a good rest. Maybe that's what we'll do. Then, when you get tired of me, you'll be right where you want to be."

For answer she just hugged me, hard.

I lay awake for a while, speculating on it all. Hell, I didn't have anything to hold me. Chulo was in San Antonio and he'd do there for a while. Wilcey seemed mighty inclined to stay with his ladylove. That left me free to run where I wanted to.

I went to sleep thinking about me and Marianne on the train together, traveling around the country. They say a woman will weaken you. I could tell Marianne was weakening me, but then I didn't care. For a time I didn't want to be Wilson Young. I'd been him so damn long I needed a recess from all the hard living that went in to being Wilson Young.

I wasn't good awake next morning when a knock came on the door. I felt Marianne stirring beside me, but I jumped out of bed, took my 44/40 out of its holster, and went to the door. As softly as I could I pulled the hammer back, it still making a faint *clitch-clatch*. I thrust out my arm, pointing my revolver at the door, about chest high. I said, "Yeah?"

Wilcey's voice came. "It's me."

"Just a minute," I said. I went back and sat down on the bed and pulled on my britches. Marianne was laying on her side, watching me. I leaned over and give her a light kiss on the mouth. "Be right back," I said. Then I went to the door, opened it, and stepped out in the hall, closing the door behind me.

Wilcey said: "She got here?"

I nodded. "Yeah."

He looked nervous. He said, "Listen, let's go to breakfast. I need to talk to you."

I said, "All right. Just wait a minute while I put some clothes on."

I stepped back in the room, closing the door behind me. Marianne said: "What?"

I said, "It's my partner, Wilcey. We're going to step next door to Delmonico's and have breakfast. He's got something he wants to talk to me about. As soon as you feel like getting up and getting dressed, you come on down there. You hear?"

She sat up, frowning. "Maybe I better not, Wilson. Maybe he wants it to be private."

I was sitting on the side of the bed pulling on my boots. I said, "No. You come. I got my own reasons for wanting you there. Don't rush, but come all the same."

"Are you sure?"

I said, "Yes." Then I turned around to her. "I trust you. I want you to understand how much I trust you. And it's been a long time since I trusted any woman. So you come down there. I ain't got any business I'd be scairt for you to hear."

She didn't say anything, just looked at me.

After I was dressed, I give her a light kiss and then went out the door and down to the lobby and then to Delmonico's. Wilcey was already at a table drinking coffee. He'd ordered a bottle of cognac, and it was sitting on the table. I sat down and the waiter brought me over a cup of coffee. I didn't say anything, nor did Wilcey, while I dressed the cup with a pretty good shot of cognac.

I tell you, there is nothing that will wake a man up in the morning faster than the smell, as he lifts it to his mouth, of those cognac fumes rising in amongst that coffee aroma. I don't believe the taste is as good as the smell. But, of course, the taste ain't bad.

But it was a kind of strange feeling to be sitting with my old partner under such circumstances. A kind of gulf had developed between us, and for the life of me I didn't know what to do about it.

I said: "You sent for breakfast yet?"

He shook his head. The waiter came over and we both ordered eggs and ham. When the waiter was gone, I said: "Well, you got a burr under your saddle blanket, or just what?"

He said: "Will, I'll come straight out with this. I want us to rob that money transfer from the bank."

I just said: "Forget it."

He said, almost pleading, "Will, think about it. Do you know that Ruth told me yesterday the pouch had sixty-five thousand dollars in it. Think of that. Sixty-five thousand dollars!"

I said dryly, "And think of what it'll cost to bury all three of us. Which is what we'll get if we try that kind of robbery." I shook my head. "No, Wilcey. We ain't going to rob that money-transfer. You want to try it, you go right ahead, and I'll give the eulogy at your graveside."

He said, "Oh, shit, Will. Don't hand me that. You know I wouldn't know how to plan a job like that. You know I wouldn't have a Chinaman's chance. But you do know all that. I've seen you. You always know how to figure a way to get the job done. Shit! You can do it."

I said, "No, I can't. And I ain't going to." I stopped speaking, for the waiter had come up with our breakfast. I waited until he left and then I said, "The reason I'm still alive is that I never took on every job that come along. Some can be done and some can't. They's plenty of men in the cemetery and in jail took on jobs couldn't be done. This is one can't be done. Get that through your head and forget this one. Houston is not a place we can do any business. I'm in favor of pulling out of here."

"No," he said, real quick. "No. We can't leave yet."

I said: "Maybe you can't, but I can."

Well, that hurt him, I could see that. Him and me had been pards a long time. I tried to soften it up a little. I said: "Hell, Dennis, stick around and have yourself a good time. I'll go off with Marianne and do the same. Then we'll join back up on the trail somewheres."

But he wasn't having any of that. "Wilson," he said, "this is a chance for me. I want that woman, I want to marry her and settle down. There's all that money just to be grabbed."

I could see I wasn't getting through to him. I leaned across the table. "Wilcey, get it straight once and for all. I ain't going to get myself killed over your goddamn woman."

He looked at me a long time. Then he said: "I almost got myself killed over yours. Or have you forgotten." He said it soft, but the words hit home like .44 shells.

He was talking about the bank robbery in Sabinas Hidalgo. I'd claimed that I'd picked that town because it had a rich bank in it. But it hadn't fooled Wilcey, for he'd heard me talk about this Linda, this little highborn senorita that I'd carried around in my head and heart for years. And he'd known that the bank was the bank that her husband was president of. And he'd known that if I was to get this Linda out of my soul, I was going to have to fuck her or rape her or see her and be able to ignore her. So he'd gone along with a bank robbery that would allow me to see her in such a way that I could do what I wanted with her. It was a plan, to say the least, that was dangerous for all concerned. Yet he and Chulo had agreed to do it the way I wanted, even at the risk of their own lives.

And, of course, it hadn't just been Linda. There had been other occasions when I'd jeopardized all our lives over a woman. Wilcey had complained, but he had never backed down on me as a friend.

Remembering made me feel a little ashamed of myself.

I said: "All right, Dennis. I understand now how important it is to you. I think you're wrong to pick this particular job."

He said: "But where would we find another with

this kind of money? And think how long we'd have to be gone and how long it would take to do it?"

I said: "I understand. You don't want to be away from Ruth that long."

He looked down. "I guess you think I'm pretty chicken shit for pushing you like this. Bringing up the past."

I shook my head. "No, I don't. I don't blame you. If anybody's chicken shit, it's me for having to be reminded how many times you put your head in the noose for me. Now let's forget it. One thing, I've got to talk to your lady friend pretty soon."

He said: "What are you going to talk to her about?"

"Oh," I said, "I just think I might can get more information out of her. Never know what might help."

He said: "You be careful, Will. Don't you get her involved."

I didn't say anything. But I had a pretty good idea ladylove knew a hell of a lot more than she was letting on to Wilcey. In fact, I was beginning to wonder who was planning the job, me or Ruth.

We ate in silence for a few minutes, and then Marianne came through the door and up to our table. She was wearing a very pretty, very sedate little ankle-length day dress. I scrambled up and pulled her over a chair. Then I introduced her to Wilcey. He was staring at her in amazement. He said, "Is this her?"

I said, "Yes, Wilcey, this is her. Now sit down and shut your mouth before you catch a fly."

He said, "Well, I'm mighty pleased to meet you, Miss Mason. I've heard considerable about you."

"I've heard about you, too, Mister Wilcey. I understand you and Will have been partners a long time."

The waiter came then, and she turned her order in for coffee and melon. Wilcey didn't stay much longer, but what time he did he just kept staring at Marianne.

I about halfway expected him to blurt out, "But, Will, she don't look like no whore." Fortunately he didn't. Though I don't reckon it would have bothered Marianne one whit.

Finally, he did leave, saying he'd see me that afternoon. It had been funny for a few minutes, but now that he was gone, the impact of what I'd agreed to do hit me. I got silent and looked down at my plate.

Marianne, seeing my mood, said, "What's wrong, Will?"

I just shook my head.

But she persisted. She put her hand on mine and said: "Something's wrong. Now tell me what it is."

I shrugged. "I've let myself get put in a box."

Chapter Six

~~~~~~

She said, "What are you talking about? What do you mean, you just got put in a box? What kind of box?"

I laughed without humor. "Maybe a burying box."

She stopped eating and put her fork down. "I don't like that kind of talk. You better tell me what you mean about all this."

I thought about not telling her, but it didn't seem to make a hell of a lot of difference. If she was going to sell me out to the law, she could already have done so.

I said, "Well, I'm going to have to try and pull a job I don't think will work, and I think it's got a good chance to get us killed." I went on and filled her in how close me and Wilcey were and how many times he'd gone along with me. Then I told her about the job.

I was talking low so that we couldn't be overheard, and she was leaning toward me. By the time I was finished she was looking more and more worried. She said, "You don't have to do it. You shouldn't do it."

I said, "I got to. I ain't got no choice."

She said, "But God, surely Wilcey can see how dangerous it would be! Do another robbery."

I shook my head. "No, this one is near and can be done quick, and he don't want to wait. He's got visions of marrying his ladylove before this afternoon or at least by Sunday. Near as I can figure. And he ain't got time for us to spend a couple of months hunting out a job and then pulling it off. The fact that he might get killed pulling this one don't seem to make him no never mind."

"But you say it can't be done. Why don't he understand that?"

I shrugged. "Because he is blinded by loooove, and he's seen me pull off enough deals that he thinks I can figure out a way to do this one."

"Then just tell him no."

I looked at her. "You don't mean that."

"Of course I do."

I shook my head. "That ain't my style, Marianne. That ain't my style at all. On this matter I ain't got no selection."

She said: "He ain't much of a friend to ask this of you."

"And that ain't true, either. God knows I've asked enough of him in the past and he's my friend. I don't know what kind of friends you got, but in my crowd it's your friends that you ask the most of. I ain't never had much luck asking enemies for favors."

We finished up breakfast and went on back to the hotel. It was around ten in the morning. I said, "Honey, can you entertain yourself for a couple of hours? I figure it's time I went out and bought some horses. We need some good horses and I ain't been in too much of a rush about it because I didn't think there was any need. Now I reckon there is."

She said: "You go ahead, cowboy. I'm just going to sleep. I've been dreaming of doing nothing but sleeping. You take your time."

I went out and hunted the horse barns. I couldn't find what I was looking for, but I knew that if we were going to pull a robbery I'd better find us some horse flesh and damn fast, for this job could come up almost at any time. Finally one of the horse traders, who seemed to have some idea that I wanted a road horse, suggested a ranch out of town about eight miles. He said: "It's near a little settlement called Roans Prairie. Just about due southwest. If anybody in this part of the country's got the kind of horses you're looking for, they'll have 'em out there. Old man Drake, it's his ranch. But he's a sonofabitch to deal with. Won't sell you a horse unless he likes you. Damn sure ain't no businessman."

Which sounded like my kind of folks. I made me a mental resolve to hie my way out to this Mister Drake's ranch the next morning. Figured I'd hire a surrey and take Marianne with me.

I thought to buy two horses, one for me and one for Wilcey. Chulo would have already found him a good mount in San Antonio. I wasn't worried about the black Mexican; he knew how to take care of himself.

I didn't see Wilcey the balance of that afternoon, nor that night, for which I was grateful. I needed to think, and I didn't need his yearning face in front of me while I was doing it. Marianne and I spent a quiet evening, had a little supper, made a little love, talked a little, and got a good night's rest.

I tell you, that woman made me feel content. I didn't quite know how to feel about it, me being who I was, a man who'd spent his life in mistrust of most men, and all women, yet this woman I'd only known a short time was becoming my friend.

We could talk together, talk plain and honest. Something I'd never done with a woman before. My mind had gone back to our earlier conversation when she'd said that Wilcey ought to be able to see how dangerous the job was. And she'd said, "Do another robbery."

Do another robbery.

Not, "Oh, my God, you're not talking about a robbery! Oh, no! Please don't rob!" With her hands up in front of her face and tears running out between her fingers.

No, she'd taken the position that I was a robber and all she wanted me to do was to have the good sense to pull the kind of robbery that had the best chance of being done without me being hurt or killed.

Ain't many women like that.

And I laid there in the bed that night, after she'd gone to sleep, thinking about what a woman she was. I didn't know what our future might shape up as, but I did know that I wanted more than just two weeks of her time.

Right after breakfast next morning I told her we were going to take a little drive in the country. "Go ahead and get a little gussied up. I hear I'm going to be dealing with an old bastard and ain't much that softens up an old bastard's heart any faster than a pretty woman."

I went around to the livery stable and hired a buggy and team, then drove around to the front of the hotel. I'd gotten good directions to old man Drake's place and figured I could find it without any trouble. Marianne, thoughtful woman that she was, was waiting on the boardwalk, and I didn't even have to tie the team and go in and get her.

We set out up the street. It was a fine spring day, with just enough sun to make it mighty pleasant. We rolled on out of town and I found the little road I'd been directed to at a crossroads about a mile out of the town limits.

I said to Marianne: "It takes a power of time to get out of that place."

She said: "There's bigger."

I slapped the team with the reins to get them to pick up the gait. "Not that I've seen," I said.

We rolled on out this country road, the rear wheels throwing up rooster tails of dust behind us. It was pretty lush country, green and flat, but it wasn't the kind of country I was used to. And the air was kind of thick and hard to breathe. I was used to a good deal higher climate.

This little settlement of Roan's Prairie wasn't where old man Drake lived. He lived off the road we were traveling about a mile on farther through the little settlement.

Marianne said: "You done any more thinking about that robbery?"

I said: "It's mostly what's been on my mind."

"Are you going to do it?"

"If I can figure out a way? I'm not going to commit suicide, if that's what you're asking. I'm going to give it my best shot for Wilcey's sake, and it might be a little more riskier than is to my liking, but if it can be done, I'm going to pull it off."

She was silent.

I said: "You didn't want to hear that?"

She said: "I just hate to see a lovely man act like a damn fool."

Now it was my turn not to talk. I just looked over at her and didn't say anything. She could either understand that a man did what he had to do or she could not understand it. It was up to her.

We raised Roan's Prairie and went wheeling on in through the few little buildings. Was a couple of townspeople out on the street, and they give us a pretty good looking over. I pulled the buggy up in front of one of them, a dirt-farmer-looking fellow wearing a black slouch hat, and asked him if he knew the way to old man Drake's place.

He looked at me for a long time, about like I'd

asked him for a loan of money, finally shifted the cud he had in his cheek, spit, and said: "Ya'll mean Horace Drake's place. On out the road a piece. First road to yer raight."

I thanked him and drove on. Me and Marianne still hadn't said anything to each other. We found the turn onto a wagon trace, and I wheeled the team there and went cantering up the lane. There was a little creek off to our right that was well lined with willow and sage and some other underbrush. I said to Marianne, carefully, "I don't much like being called a fool. If you feel like not sticking around to see me act like one, then I'll put you on the next train you say."

She said a little stiffly, "Cowboy, I reckon I'm big enough to catch a train on my own. I don't need your help."

Well, goddamnit, I didn't see no call for her to be getting stiff-necked with me. I said: "Then maybe you ought to. Since you think I'm a fool. Big girl like you wouldn't want to be around any fools."

About then we swept under an arched gate and I could see a house sitting up like a monument on the flat prairie. "That'd be it," I said.

She didn't say anything.

As we got closer I could see some corrals and a few outbuildings. It wasn't a really duded-up outfit, but it had the solid look of a place that wasn't worried about the banker coming to call with your note in his hand. As we got closer I could see the house was a solid affair and that the outbuildings and corrals were well tended and in good repair. I went straight on up to the front of the house. I would have liked to have swung by the corrals and seen the quality of livestock, but that ain't considered real polite when you're on a man's property.

I got to the front of the house, got out, tied the

team, bade Marianne to wait, and then clumped up to the big wooden door and knocked. Nothing happened so I knocked again. I hadn't seen a soul around the place, and I wasn't real sure anyone was home.

I stood there, kind of idly admiring the woodwork on the door and slapping at the dust on my breeches with my hat and waiting. All of a sudden the door was flung open. I was expecting, given the size of the place, that some sort of a servant would be coming. But, instead, it was a tall, gaunt old man with whiskers and hair flying in every direction that was standing in the opening. He was wearing an old white shirt without a collar and a black vest with a gold watch chain across the front and black stovepipe britches.

He give me a look that hadn't a bit of welcome in it. Then he said, "Well, what the hell you want?"

I said: "I'm looking for Horace Drake."

He give me a hard eye. "Yeah, and what would you be wanting with him?"

I put my hat on. I said, "I hear he's got good horses. Which I doubt. If I can find him I'm looking to buy a couple of good road horses off him."

He looked past my shoulder, at the buggy with Marianne in it. Then he swung back to me. "What the hell would you want with good road horses? You got a pretty little buggy there to ride in."

I said: "That's just for Sunday drives. Actually I'm a bank robber, and I need a couple of good road horses to outrun the catch party that's generally after me. Now listen, you old bastard, you want to direct me to Horace Drake? Or, if you're him, you want to either come out or let me in so we can discuss business?"

I was about half mad, and no mistake. He give me

a long look then kind of cackled. "Wal by God, you be a plainspoken one, ain't you?"

I said: "Are you Drake?"

"That be me."

I told him my name was Jim Wilson and put out my hand, which he took in his old bony fist. I said: "You got good horses for sale?"

"I got good horses. Depends on whether a man knows a good horse if they be for sale."

I said, "I'll know. But I'll need to see them sometime before winter comes."

He cackled again. "Then you'd best come in and have a morning whiskey. My horses is not to be appreciated on a dry stomach." He looked past me again, at the buggy, at Marianne. He said, "Your lady be coming in?"

I said, "Yes," and went and fetched her from the buggy. On the porch I introduced her as "Missus Wilson," and then we followed the old man into a parlor.

It was obvious he lived alone, or alone without a wife, for the place sure didn't show a woman's touch. It wasn't all that bad, but a wife generally won't put up with a man slinging a couple of saddles in the corner of the sitting room or leaving bottles of whiskey standing all over the place or spurs laying on top of the vanity table or underwear on the divan.

Drake said: "Ya'll set. And what'll be your pleasure?"

Marianne and I sat on the divan, side by side, me choosing the end with the underwear. I crossed my knees and put my hat on my knee. "I'll take whatever you have, whiskey or brandy or rum or whatever."

He said, "Got 'em all. Ain't nobody ever been able to come to Horace Drake's 'n' ask for a drink I ain't got. What about the missus?"

Marianne said: "I'll have a brandy."

"We'll make it three," Drake said. He went out of the room, to the kitchen I suppose, and came back with three glasses, one of which he was wiping out with the tail of his shirt. I didn't mind that. I figured the brandy he had would kill any kind of varmit under a pound. He poured out all around and then we all said, "Luck," and knocked them straight back as befits the toast. Then he poured out again and we settled back.

I said: "You deal mostly in horses, Mister Drake?"

He said: "Pretty much. I do considerable business with some freighting outfits in Houston, and I'm a contractor to the United States calvary for trooper mounts."

I said, "I'd be looking for a better class of horse than that."

He shot me a quick look. "I understood that from you from the first, sir. What you may not understand is that I ain't agreed yet to sell you a goddamn horse. It'll be your blood lines will be inspected first."

Well, I had to laugh at the old gentleman. He damn sure might have been old, but he hadn't lost none of his buck. I said, "Well, how the hell we going to do that?"

He said: "You be from Houston?"

I said: "No. Just stopping off there until I can get remounted and move out."

He snorted. "Well, that by God is a mark in your favor. Not being from that goddamn Yankee town." He glanced toward Marianne. "Asking your pardon, missus. I'm an old man not been used to women an' I tend to be a bit plainspoken."

She said, giving him a look, "Just cuss all the goddamn hell you please."

Which made him throw back his head and laugh.

I said: "Don't worry about the lady. Let's see the horses."

He stopped his laugh, cut it short, and looked at me. "What makes you think I'd sell you horses?"

"Maybe you ain't got the kind I'm looking to buy."

He tugged at his collar, kind of opening his shirt, and leaned forward in his chair. "Let's you and me get something straight there, mister. I got the kind of horses *you're* looking for." He gestured. "Don't reckon that Horace Drake don't know a man by the set of his gun, and I see how yours is set up on your laig. I understand you all the way, young sir. You may have thought you was hoorahing me about being a bank robber, but it may be I know a bit more about you than you think."

Well, that scared me a little bit, him figuring me so quick. Of course I wasn't about to admit it. I said, "Yeah, you know all about me. Likely you've furnished the mounts for Wes Harding and Jesse James."

He gave me that sharp-eyed look. "Don't be so sure about that, young fool. Especially Jesse James. I come here from Missouri right after the Civil War. And the bloodlines of my horses go back to Clay County in Missouri."

Well, that was twice in one day I'd been called a fool. Worse, Marianne had laughed when the old man said it. I turned and give her a look, intending she was to keep her goddamn mouth shut. Especially if she was going to use it to laugh at me.

I also done it so the old man wouldn't read any interest on my face. What he'd just said about Clay County horses was true. The bloodline, even a little of it, was highly prized by men who knew horses. I'd mostly heard about it, only having had the chance to own one, a big bay I'd ridden for two years only to lose him in a flight from a bank robbery.

But I was a good deal interested in the old man's favorable attitude toward people in my profession. Of course, he could be selling me, but I didn't think so, and a man in my line of work very often has to go on his feelings for people. But I had to be a little more sure before I was going to admit much. I said: "You say you came here right after the Civil War?"

He nodded, a little stiffly.

I said: "Which side was you on? Yankee?"

Well, I thought he was going to explode. His face swelled up and he got red around the wattles. He burst out: "By God, sir, you make that remark again and I'll shoot you down like a dog! In spite of the fact yore pistol is set up like a gunfighter's!"

I said: "Well, you can see it was an honest mistake. I knew you wasn't a Texan. That was plain, though I don't hold it against you. A man that ain't born a Texan has got enough of a hardship without being reminded of it. But, considering the degree of your hospitality, I had no selection but to figure you for a Yankee. You will admit it's a little slack for a southerner."

He stared at me. Then he opened his mouth and shut it. Finally he said, "Why damn your cheek!" Then he laughed. He said: "Well, by God, maybe I had that acomin'. Maybe I did. Old men sometimes get set in their ways and get a little cranky." He got up. "Let's take another drink and then I'll show you my horses. Might be I'll even sell you one."

Well, we had that other drink and then he and I went on out to the corrals, leaving Marianne to entertain herself in the parlor.

Walking out the old man said: "Mighty pretty missus you got thar."

I said, "Thanks."

He said: "How does a man in yore profession come to be married?"

I said, "You're a nosy old parker, ain't you."

He cackled. "Ain't often I get me a pretty lady and a robber in the same package."

I said: "How you know she ain't the robber?"

"Wal, don't reckon she'd need a gun. Nor a get-away horse neither."

I didn't have a plan set in my mind yet as to how I could pull the robbery off. But I knew I was going to need more help than I presently had. And this old man might just be help.

I still needed to know more about him, though.

But I held my tongue while we walked up to a pen of six or seven horses that I guessed I was to inspect for purchase. I could see with one eye the old man was testing me. They was good stock, but they were over the hill. I mouthed one just to be sure and the horse was an easy ten-year-old. Another one had a gimpy cannon bone. I didn't know who old man Drake planned to sell these horses to, but I knew it wasn't going to be me. I didn't say anything, just dusted off my hands. The old man cackled and we walked around a barn to where another pen of horses was collected in a little corral. As we walked I asked the old man if he lived alone.

He had taken a chaw of tobacco and he took time to spit. Then he said, "No, my oldest boy, Amos, and I kind of batch together. My old woman died ten years ago. Got a brother he'ps us run the place, but he's over to the army post between here and Fort Worth doing a little business."

I said, "Just you and your boy run this big operation?"

He give me a look like he knew I was probing him. But he said, "No, I just got two white hands and one Mexican." Then, just like he was reading my mind, he said: "All of 'em been with me a right smart time and they mighty trusty."

We came to the next pen and I could see they were

better horses, but still a far piece from what I had in mind. Still I crawled through the bars of the corral and looked in a few mouths and inspected a few feet and felt a few legs and hams. The old man was watching me pretty hard. When I was through, I just looked at him. I was beginning to wonder if I was going to have to look at every horse on the place before he showed me what I wanted, but then he said, "All right. Com'on."

Well, we walked on past about two more corrals of horses, and at the end of the line was one with six mounts in it, any one of which, I could see from twenty yards away, would be what I was looking for. I went on into the corral and mouthed a couple of them. They were all what they looked, honest four-year-olds. You could see the breeding in them. Breeding don't always mean that much, but in these horses it meant blood and blood meant staying power. I kept on looking them over. They were iron hard, clean limbed, and as well shod as any horses I'd ever seen. I picked a bay gelding about sixteen and a half hands high for myself and a roan of about the same size for Wilcey. Then I walked over to where old man Drake was leaning with his arms over the corral fence. He said, "Well, what ya think?"

I lit a cigarillo. "They'll do. What are you asking?"

He spit again. "Two fifty a head. And that's only because I done taken a liking to you."

Well, it was damn high for horseflesh, in any part of the country. But they weren't your ordinary horses and they was worth it to me. I said, "Done. For two head. The bay gelding with the white stocking on the left front foot and the roan gelding with the blazed face."

He gave the corral a quick glance. "Well, you've taken my two best. I'd of said three hundred if I'd knowed you was that smart. You don't want to sling a saddle on one? Take a little ride."

I shook my head. "Nope. Not these kind of horses. And I don't need the practice."

He cackled and we started walking back in to the house. He said, "We'll get a drink and then come out and put a lead rope on 'em and tie 'em to the back of yore buggy."

I said: "I might not want to take them with me today. I'm thinking on something else."

"What would that be?"

I said: "Let me pay you first and have that drink while I study on it."

We went on in and Marianne was sitting where we'd left her. She'd located herself a fan, and she was sitting there fanning herself with it. Drake said: "I trust you've passed the time profitably, ma'am."

I said: "He damn sure has. Just got through holding me up for two horses."

He raised his bristly old eyebrows. "Don't feel obligated to take them, sir."

I said, "Hell, you look like you need the money."

We poured out again, though Marianne declined, saying it was too hot for much brandy. But me and the old man knocked ours back, and then I got out my wallet and counted him out five hundred dollars in gold certificates.

"Just lay it on that little table," he said, gesturing. "Now, what other business you got to jaw with me about?"

He'd sat down in a chair across from me, and I halfway felt like the old fool knew what I wanted to talk about. But I waited to get myself another drink and to sit back down by Marianne. I glanced at her, she was watching old man Drake, a slight smile on her face. I said to Drake, "Tell me, horse trader, you made mention of Houston being a Yankee town awhile back. Didn't you study your geography when you was at your books? Houston is in Texas."

"Pshaw!" he said. "Houston is more Yankee than it is Texan! A'ter the Civil War ever' goddamn carpetbagger and scalawag in the country headed for Houston. It's a damn Babylon! And I'll have no part of it!"

"Then why you live this close?"

He said, and struck himself in the chest as he did so, "Because, by God, sir, I was here first!"

"But you said you come here after the Civil War."

"And that's a fact! But this by God land was here! A grant to my pappy, who passed it on to me!"

Well, the old man felt strongly about the matter and no mistake. I said, "You took five hundred dollars for them two horses. What would you take to give, uh, well, let's say, a place to rest up for three hombres?"

The old man narrowed his eyes. He said, "One of them hombres be you?"

I nodded. "Yeah. Me and two others. Two, at most three days."

He stared at me hard, and for a moment I thought I'd made a mistake. Then he said: "You and your friends be riding in here with your horses whipped to a froth and a crowd of people following you across the prairie?"

I shook my head. "Nope. Won't be nobody nipping at our heels. Not if everything goes right. And if it don't go right, why then I don't reckon we'd be coming this way at all. However, if our business goes right, there's going to be some folks considerably interested in our whereabouts, and that's a little secret we'd like to keep to ourselves."

He rubbed his chin. "Where you thinking on doing this business?"

I held out my hands, palms up. "Houston, where else?"

He cackled. "So there was a rhyme to your reasoning out my hate for that infernal town."

"Well, what about it? Would you do it?"

He rubbed his jaw again and glanced at Marianne. "You allus talk so free in front of your mistress?"

I laughed dryly. "You ought to hear what she says in front of me. No, she knows my business. Keeps her from thinking I'm with other women when I'm away nights."

He didn't cackle at that, just rubbed his chin again and scratched at his scraggly mustache. He said, "You say they won't be no catch party riding in here right after you?"

I shook my head. "No. That'd be part of the condition. I want to leave those two good horses here. One of my friends will already be well mounted and he'll go on on his horse. My other friend and myself will leave our two animals here with you and go on on the two good horses I bought from you."

He raised his head. "These two you be leaving. They wouldn't be stolen?"

I gave him a disgusted look. "Hell, old man, I'm a robber, not a horse thief. No, they're worthless nags we bought in Galveston some few weeks back. Good to look at, but ain't fit for men in our line of work."

He nodded and got up and poured us more brandy. I sipped at mine. "Well?"

"When would this be?"

"Soon," I said. "I can't give you a day. Just when you see us coming. How about your son and your hired hands? They trustworthy?"

He give me that fierce look again. "Ain't a man on this place ain't part of the place. Whatever this place takes on to do every man will back it!"

I nodded. The talk had turned serious. I glanced at

Marianne. She wasn't smiling anymore. I said, "Well, will you agree to do it?"

He said: "Done. You and your two friends come here. You'll be safe for two or three days."

I said, "How much?"

He shook his head. "We'll not talk on that now. Wait and see how your business goes. Might be you can't pay anything."

I said: "I don't much like that. I'd rather settle a price now."

He got up. "Won't do it. Just take it that Horace Drake is an honest man. I like your style, sir. Leave it at that."

We walked out to the porch together, and he insisted on helping Marianne into the buggy. He said, "Ain't often an old man gets to touch a pretty young missus."

I got in and he said: "Yore horses will be waiting."

I said: "Be ready for us, old man." Then I wheeled the buggy and drove back out the lane, heading for Houston.

Marianne didn't say anything for a good little while. Neither did I, my mind busy trying to figure out the details of a plan that was beginning to form in my mind about how to rob that transfer agent. Finally, she said: "What makes you so sure you can trust that old man?"

I said: "I ain't sure. Fact of the business is I ain't sure about anything. What makes me sure I can trust you?" I glanced at her. She didn't say anything, just stared back at me with those blue eyes. I slapped the horses with the reins. "You go into this business you early on find out they ain't nothing sure. It's all a risk. From time to time you've got to trust a few people. I've been uncommonly lucky in having damn few of them turn on me. That's the best I can tell you."

"How come you think you'll need the old man? What do ya'll want a hideout at his ranch for?"

I shrugged. "Marianne, a job like this you start out just trying to use the materials at hand. I ain't got no definite plan in mind yet, just some ideas, and some of them might change. I ain't even sure yet I'm going to need old man Drake, all I got is an idea I might."

She went a ways farther not saying anything, then she said: "So you've decided to do it. You're going ahead with this fool's robbery."

I pulled the horses up so hard she almost slid off the seat. I looked around at her. She was staring straight ahead. "Now listen, little lady, and listen carefully. I don't know what the hell's got into you, but you've called me a fool for the last time."

Hell, I couldn't figure out what was the matter with her. Ever since I'd told her about the robbery Wilcey wanted to do, she'd turned sour. Well, I'd never been able to figure women, and I didn't see no reason why I ought to start at my present age. So I just whipped up the horses and we drove on to Houston in silence.

I let her out at the front of the hotel and then drove around back to the livery stable to return the buggy and team. When I got back up to the room, she was sitting on the bed, her hands in her lap, wearing just her shift and hose. I never said a word. Just walked over to the bowl, poured out some water, washed my face, and then poured myself a drink. Then I sat down in a chair opposite her. She just sat there, looking down at her hands. I sipped at my drink. I had a bad feeling what was about to come. Well, she wouldn't be the first woman ever deserted me. Hell, if she didn't, she'd be the exception.

I took the time, before I spoke, to take off my gun belt and hang it over a knob on the back of the chair. It had come good afternoon and the room was warm.

I got up and raised a window. When I sat back down, I said, "Looks like summer is coming. And no mistake."

She didn't say anything.

I knew what she was working up to tell me, and, I tell you, it put a ball in the pit of my stomach. What made it hurt worse was that I'd thought, once I was all through with that little highborn senorita, that I was over that kind of foolishness. But here I was, waiting for the fateful sentence from a whore.

A whore! By God! A whore!

Well, I commenced getting angry. It seemed that this had been done to me enough, and I was getting damned tired of it. I said, an edge in my voice, "Well, why don't you get on with it? What the hell is holding you up?

She finally looked up at me. "What?"

I said: "Get on with it." I gestured at her with my glass of brandy. "You ain't going to hurt my feelings. As a matter of fact I ain't going to be a damn bit disappointed."

She said: "What in the hell are you talking about?"

"Don't play the calf with me, Marianne. I know what's been going through that head of yours ever since you found out about this robbery Wilcey wants me to pull. First you argued against it. When you seen that wouldn't work, why then you sulled up. And now that that ain't going to work, I know what your next step is going to be. Well, go ahead and take it!" I put the brandy to my mouth and downed it at a gulp.

She was looking at me, her head cocked to the side. Now that she was leaving she looked prettier than ever. "I asked you, what the hell are you talking about?"

I said, plenty angry now, for now she was playing

me for the calf, I said, "You. You're leaving. Well, so what! If you've missed your train, I'm sure you can find another bed to lay in until the next one pulls out of the depot."

Chapter Seven

~~~~~~

She said, "You're a goddamn fool." She said it flatly and boldly, even after I'd told her she'd better not ever call me such a thing again.

I got quiet inside. I said: "You better watch your mouth, woman."

"Is that what you think, that I'm fixing to run out on you?"

"What the hell else am I supposed to think?" I got up and walked over to the little table and poured me some brandy. When I sat back down she was still looking at me. I said, "Yeah, what the hell else am I supposed to think?"

She commenced to get angry. I could see it in her face. "Well, if you think that, you can goddamn well go to hell! And stay there! You sonofabitch!"

Well, I was that surprised. The damn woman was one too many for me. Hell, I was the one supposed to be mad. And here she was cussing me out. I said, "Well, if you ain't leaving, you'd be the first goddamn woman I ever seen didn't run out on me when the going got a little rough."

She said, and I tell you, her voice was cold, "I ain't every woman."

I said: "You couldn't prove that by me."

She said, "That does it." She got up and began

jerking her clothes out of the closet and throwing them on the bed. I didn't say a word. Over her shoulder she said, "I don't know what put it into your head that I was leaving because I wasn't. Now I wouldn't stay if you paid me!"

I said, "Oh, yes you would. You're a whore, ain't you? You'll do anything for money."

She said, "Goddamn you!" and flung what looked to be a whalebone corset at my head. I dodged just in time and then, to my great surprise, she suddenly burst out crying. Well, it taken me aback. I didn't know what to say. She went on jerking clothes out of the closet, crying and saying, "Oh, you sonofabitch! Oh, you sonofabitch!"

I said, "Well, now look here! What is all this? If you wasn't planning on leaving, how come you got all sulled up? If ever I seen a woman looking for a way to say adios it was you."

She just went on wrecking the closet and crying. I said: "Well, goddamnit! Can't you answer me?"

Then she turned around to face me, her hands on her hips, tears rolling down her cheeks. "You dumb bastard, did it ever enter that mule's brain of yours that I might have been worrying about you? You're supposed to be so smart, was that I was going to leave all you could figure out?"

I said, kind of uncertainly, "Well, I never thought. I mean, I didn't know what else to think. I—"

"That's right, you never thought. You never seen how much I cared for you, and I didn't want to see you get your fool head blowed off."

"Cared for me?"

"Aw, go to hell!" she said. "What's the use?" She turned back to the closet. "Goddamn man. Ain't no different from any other."

I didn't know what to do or to say. I'd never run

into such a situation in all my born days. Finally, I said, "Marianne."

She didn't answer me. I said, "Marianne."

She drug her suitcase out of the closet and slung it on the bed. I got up and went over to her. She had her back to me. I put my hands on her waist and turned her around. She wouldn't look up at me. I said, "Don't go."

Then she looked up in my face. She said, "Go to hell!" She was still crying.

I got a little angry. I said, "What the hell you want me to do, beg you?"

"Yes," she said. "Beg me."

Goddamn she looked pretty, her hair all golden and her breasts swelling out of the bodice of her shift. I said, "All right, I'm begging. Marianne, don't go. Please don't go."

She continued to look up in my face. "Why not?"

"Because I don't want you to. I want you with me."

She didn't say nothing, just put her arms around my neck, pulled my head down, and kissed me. Then she pulled back and said, "But don't you ever talk to me like that again, or I will leave."

We went to bed then and I don't guess I'd ever known what sweet lovemaking was until that afternoon. I took all the tenderness I had in my soul and gave it to her, but I felt like I was getting back more than I gave, no matter how hard I tried. Before it was over there wasn't an inch of her body that I didn't know, and there wasn't an inch of mine she didn't know. I'd never been kissed and caressed so much in my life. When the end finally came we both just kind of slipped into sleep. We awoke with the shadows getting long in the room. I raised up on an elbow, trying not to disturb her, and looked out the window. It was coming dusk. Then I lay back down beside her, holding her close.

After a time she said: "Do you know what you're going to do next, honey? About the robbery?"

I said, "I'm starting to kind of work up a plan."

"Want to talk about it?"

"No. I never talk about it until I've got it all straight in my head. Parts of it are still bothering me." I got up on an elbow so I could look down in her face. "Are you going to stay with me? I might need you for a little part of it."

She said, "I'm not going to leave unless you run me off."

I said, "Well, you sure scared the hell out of me the last day or so. I figured for sure you were fixing to light a shuck."

She sighed. "Yeah, I guess I did act kind of silly. Give me a drink of that brandy."

I handed her the glass. She sipped and then she said, "Looks like a woman who's been around as much as I have wouldn't be trying to tell a man his business. You were an outlaw when I met you. Looks like I'd have sense enough to take you as you are and not worry you by worrying about you. You were right. I was sulking. It won't happen again."

Wasn't a hell of a lot I could say. I'd never known a woman to talk like that before. Finally, I just said, "Aw, I guess I kind of boiled the pot a little too much. Here, give me a drink of that brandy, woman."

I lit a cigarillo and kind of hiked my back up there on the pillow and then lay there smoking and thinking.

She said, "What's next?"

"I got to talk to Wilcey's woman."

"What for?"

"Well, I'm playing a hunch about her. But I got to do it, for, best I can figure, without her they ain't going to be any way to pull this job off."

She sat up. She said, a little alarm in her voice,

"Will, what are you talking about? You're not going to tell that woman what you're planning? My God, she doesn't know that you and Wilcey are outlaws! You tell her anything and she's liable to go to the police."

I shrugged. "It ain't as much of a chance as it sounds like. I got a strong feeling about that little lady, even though I've never met her. One I'm most worried about is Wilcey. He ain't going to like what I got in mind worth a damn."

"What are you going to talk to her about?"

"Tell you when I get it all worked out." I got out of bed and started dressing. "Get your fat ass out of bed, woman. I'm hungry. Let's go eat us some oysters. I think you got every oyster I had built up in me. That is, if what they say is true."

We went out and had a nice time. We'd been in Houston a good while by then, and while there hadn't been any trouble so far, it was just a question of time before somebody came along and recognized me. No, I was beginning to get nervous about hanging around so long. If we was going to do robbery, we was going to have to do it in a hurry and then shake the dust of the place off our heels before it was too late.

I knocked on Wilcey's door next morning and he was there so I routed him out to go to breakfast. Over our coffee he asked me what I'd come up with. Before I answered I took a good look at him across the table. His face was drawn and his eyes a little bloodshot and puffy. I said, "Well, I can see that looove is really agreeing with you. A few more weeks of this and you won't have to worry about getting married. Any woman that was going to marry you would already be a widow."

He said, "Hell, Will, don't hoorah me. You know how I feel about Ruth. I think about her all the

time. I can't eat, I can't sleep. Hell!" He turned his
head, looking miserable.

I said, "Well, from a sixteen-year-old mooncalf
that'd sound just fine. You ought to hear it coming
out of you."

His face went beet red. He said, a little touch of
anger in his voice. "All right. You're supposed to be
my friend. But you wait and see if I ever tell you another goddamn thing." He motioned to the waiter to
bring him some brandy for his coffee.

I said, "By the way, I got to talk to Ruth."

He swiveled his head back to me. "You got to talk
to Ruth? What the hell for?"

I said, "I need to talk to her about the robbery."
Knowing there was no way I could sweeten it or set
him up for it.

Well, you'd of thought, from the look on his face,
that I'd just jammed a cocked revolver between his
eyes. He said, "The helllll you will!" He half rose out
of his chair, staring at me as if I'd lost my mind.
Then he suddenly sat back down and shook his head.
"Aw, com'on, Wilson, quit hoorahing me. I never
hoorahed you as bad about your women as you have
me about Ruth."

I leaned toward him, my voice low, but intense. "I
ain't hoorahing you, Wilcey."

"Cut it out, Will. Goddamn, enough is enough."

"Listen," I said, "I'm serious. Ruth has got to help
us if we're going to do this robbery. You understand?
So I've got to talk to her."

It finally got through to him. His mouth fell open
and he dropped the fork he'd just picked up. "Wilson,
you're out of your goddamn mind! No, sir! No, sir!
No, sir!" He commenced shaking his head back and
forth. "No way, no, sir!"

I just sat there, letting him run down. Then I said:
"Wilcey, you want to pull this robbery?"

He was still shaking his head. "You ain't talking to Ruth. You ain't involving her."

I said, "Why not, I'm going to use Marianne."

"What? Man, you are crazy. Did you tell that whore about this robbery?"

"You better watch your mouth, Wilcey."

"Well, you don't be putting a whore and Ruth in the same herd, either."

"Just what makes you so goddamn sure this Ruth is such a goddamn prize? What do you know about her, anyway? Except what she's told you."

He said, "I just know. I can tell."

"Yeah, sure," I said. "You're such a goddamn good judge of females. Sure, your record proves that, don't it." It was a low thing to say, reminding him of how his wife had run out on him. I was sorry the second I said it. He put his head down and stared at his plate.

"All right," I said. "I shouldn't have said that. I'm sorry. It was a chickenshit thing to say."

He picked up his coffee cup and drank, not looking at me.

"Listen, finish your breakfast and let's take a walk up the street."

He said, "I ain't hungry no more."

"Then let's go." I paid the bill and we got up and walked outside. The streets were already busy, people hurrying all over the place. I never had got used to the air in Houston. Seemed like you damn near had to fight to get a breath. And sometimes the fog would roll in so thick you near could slice it with a knife.

We walked on up the street, not saying anything. Wilcey had his head down. I wasn't near through with him, but he didn't know that. All I was doing was giving him a chance to recover from my ill-considered remark about his record with women.

But I knew I was right about Ruth. I just naturally felt it from what Wilcey had told me.

Finally, we come to a saloon I was familiar with and I said, "Let's turn in here. I need a whiskey."

"Yeah," he said. "Myself."

We went on in. It was pretty deserted, even as late in the morning as it was. But Houston had never struck me as much of a drinking town. Seemed like everybody was too busy doing business, trying to make money. Well, we tried to make money too, but that never stopped us from having a sociable drink every now and again.

We got a table back against the wall, far enough from anyone so that we could talk in private.

After the bartender had brought us over a bottle and a couple of glasses, I poured out for us and then we knocked them back for "luck."

When a few minutes had passed, I said, "Wilcey, I got to talk to Ruth."

He looked at me, kind of sad-eyed. "Will, are you going to start that again?"

"Listen, Wilcey, the only way to pull this job off is with Ruth's help. I've thought about it from every angle, and they just ain't no other way."

"Will, to begin with, she ain't going to help us. She's a lady, not a robber."

I didn't say anything to that, though I had my own ideas.

He said, "And so the only thing you'd accomplish by talking to her would be to give me away to her as a robber. Then she'd be through with me. We been friends a long time, Will, and we been in some tight spots together. Would you do that to me? Would you foul me up like that?"

I said, "Aww, goddamnit, Wilcey. You are blinded by love. She's going to find out about you sooner or later. Why not now, before it's too late. You know you could be wrong about the little lady."

"You keep saying she's going to find out about me. That don't necessarily have to follow."

"Why not? Say we do pull this robbery without saying anything to her. Then you just suddenly disappear. You reckon she's going to think that's just a hell of a coincidence?"

He said: "I already been thinking on that. I've been telling her I might have to take off any day on a cattle-buying trip."

"Then what?" I said. "So we pull the robbery and you're off somewhere. You going to come back to Houston to fetch her? With every law in town looking for you?"

He said, kind of lowly, "I thought I could just send for her."

"And she won't think that's strange? That you can't come back to Houston? That you can't come back and help her settle her affairs and get her provender moved?"

"Maybe not. Hell, Will, quit pushing me, damnit! I ain't got your brain. I'm still trying to muddle all this out."

"Aw, shit, Wilcey!" I said. I hit the table with my fist, making the bottle and glasses jump and drawing a look from the bartender. I was that disgusted. I killed what whiskey was in my glass and poured myself out another drink. I swear to God, I almost didn't recognize my old partner anymore. He wasn't himself at all.

I said: "Have you been talking marriage to her?"

He kind of half nodded. "Yeah. Some."

"And what does she say?"

He hesitated. "Listen, this is my personal business."

"No, it ain't," I said with a little heat. "Not when you ask me to pull a job that I think is a bad risk. And you ask me to do it over some woman. It ain't your personal business no more. Now what does she say about marriage?"

He looked uncomfortable. He said: "Well, she says she cares about me, but she can't give me a straight-out yes right now."

"Why not?"

"Well, uh, on account of some debts she's got."

"What kind of debts?"

"Well, just some stuff she had before. See, Will, she's that kind of woman. She don't want to saddle me with burdens she had before we met."

I nearly fell out of my chair. That was about as disgusting a dodge as I'd ever heard. And Wilcey was falling for it hook, line, and sinker.

I said, "Wilcey, that woman knows you're an outlaw."

He took a drink of whiskey. "She knows no such thing. She believes what I told her. That I'm a cattle buyer."

"Bullshit! Wilcey, at one time you might have passed for a cattle buyer, but not no more. Not on close inspection like she's give you. You look like what you are now. You look like me. Ain't you noticed how men glance at us on the street and give us a little more room than necessary? What the hell, have your brains addled?"

He said: "Listen, and I mean this. I don't want to talk about Ruth no more. I'm sorry you ever found out about her."

I didn't want to say it, but I did. "Wilcey, she's playing you. And she's been playing you from the first."

"What the hell are you talking about? Goddamn you, Will, will you quit confusing Ruth with that whore of yours?"

"At least I got an *honest* whore."

"What's that supposed to mean?"

"Just what it sounds like. Ruth's been playing you from the first. That little lady knows what you are. And she's counting on you being damn good at it. Hell, she's done everything but come out and ask you to rob that transfer agent."

He just looked at me with those sad eyes and then slowly shook his head.

"Goddamnit, Wilcey, everything I know about that transfer agent I found out from her through you. She knows I'm running the outfit, and it's as if she was sending me messages through you. And every time you and I've had a falling out she's sent you back to make up with me. You think she did that because she's worried I might not want to breakfast the next morning if we didn't kiss and make up? Hell no, you damn fool. And remember, she don't even know me. All she knows is what you've told her about me, and I bet that's been plenty. When you're in love, you ain't got no more control over your mouth than a dog baying at the moon."

I seen it sink into him, seen him recollecting what I was talking about, seen him remembering all what she'd said and what he'd told her. Seen it in his eyes how she kept bringing up that transfer agent.

I said: "Didn't it ever strike you as funny how much she talked about the transfer of that money? Even down to the amounts? Didn't ya'll have something better to talk about? I never been spooning with no gal and all we could think of was money coming from one place to the next."

It was sinking in deeper and deeper, but he just kind of growled, "Listen, that don't prove nothing."

"It don't?" I sat back in my chair, letting him chew it over himself. His brains was addled, and no mistake, but he was still a long way from being dumb. Even at his worse.

Finally, I said: "Wilcey, as your best friend, for

your own sake, you got to find out about this woman now. She's got to know who you are, what you do. If you don't find out about her now, and she finds out about you later, you will come to grief."

He said: "But she don't have to find out about me."

"Aw, shit," I said in disgust. "Goddamnit, you are known to ride with me, and I'm wanted everywhere there is to be wanted. After Houston they ain't a place in Texas where you could settle down. Believe me, I know. Sooner or later somebody is going to come along and recognize you and then it's all up."

"We'll leave the state. Go somewheres else?"

"Where? California? Remember we done tried that. And with a hell of a power of money more than you got now. And how long did that last? Less than two years."

"I'll find someplace."

"And do what? Old hat, you're too long out of the honest man's game to ride that horse again. I tell you flatly, your only chance with that woman is to lay your cards out. Then if she takes you you'll know you got something. Otherwise you're going to be a blowed-up sucker." I sat back. I'd said all I knew to say. Now it was up to him.

He asked me for a cigarillo and I handed him one. Then he got a lucifer match out of his pocket and lit up and sat there smoking. I poured us both out a drink of whiskey while he stared off across the saloon through a blue haze of smoke.

Finally he looked over at me. He looked miserable. He said, "They ain't no other way?"

I shook my head. "No. Without Ruth's help we cannot pull that job, not with any chance of success. If you don't want me to talk with her, of course I won't. But then I'll saddle up and leave Houston. I'm already worried that we've stayed too long, and I'm expecting to be recognized at any moment."

He drew on his cigarillo, thinking. He said, "There'd be no danger to her, would there?"

I said, "None. She would be nowhere near the scene of the robbery when it happens."

"When would you want to talk to her?"

"As quick as possible. This evening, right after she gets off from work."

"That soon, huh." He swallowed. I guess he was about as scared as I'd ever seen him. But, then, I'd never seen him care so much about anyone or anything before.

We'd been at this talk about two hours, and I was beginning to get impatient. In the first place, I didn't even want to do the robbery; I was only doing it for Wilcey. And here he was, being the logjam. But, hell, I could understand how he felt. He was my partner and he wasn't thinking too good. I had to do it for him.

I said, "Com'on, Wilcey, make up your mind."

"All right," he finally said. Then he sighed and looked over at me. "I hope to hell you know what you're doing. If this blows me up with Ruth, I honest to God don't know how I'm going to feel about you, Will. Whether I'll want to ride with you anymore."

"That's up to you, Wilcey. All I can tell you is that she'd of found out about you sooner or later. Better early if she's going to shuck you."

We got up and went outside. I asked Wilcey when he'd seen Ruth again.

"We're planning on eating a bite together at her house at the noon hour."

I nodded. "All right. Tell her you and I'll be over there pretty early. About five thirty this evening. I'm going back to the hotel."

He said, "Damn, Will, you sure know how to fuck up a man's morning."

I just looked at him and walked on back to the hotel.

Marianne was not in our room, and for a second I had such a stab of fear that I stepped to the closet to see that her clothes were still there. Well, that made me laugh. I was acting just like Wilcey. I poured myself out a brandy and sat down in the chair in front of the window that fronted on main street. I didn't much like the way Wilcey called Marianne a whore and seemed to think that she wasn't fit to be mentioned in the same breath with Ruth. But I figured I'd just chalk it up to love and inexperience. As far as I was concerned I'd about had my fill of them fine ladies who seemed to have all the habits of a dog except loyalty.

I just continued to sit there, staring out the window, smoking and drinking and trying to make some details of the robbery plan fit in. After about an hour the door opened and Marianne come in with a bunch of packages in her arms. She'd been out shopping. She kissed me and then said, "Oh, I bought you a present."

I said, "What?"

She said, "I bought you a present." She put her packages down on the bed and then took up one and unwrapped it. Then she turned around, holding it out in front of her. "A silk shirt!"

Well, I was that taken aback that I didn't know what to say. To the best of my knowledge no woman, outside of my mother, had ever give me anything except a hard time. I didn't know what to say.

She said: "Now take off that shirt you're wearing. I want to see if it fits so I can take it back if it don't."

Well, nothing would do her but I get up and take off my shirt and put on the one she'd bought for me.

It was a deep blue and you could see with one eye it was a fine piece of goods. I didn't reckon I'd ever owned a silk shirt before. And it wasn't that I didn't have the money; it's just not the kind of thing a man would think to buy for himself.

I finally said, "Hell, Marianne, you kind of took me off guard. I am much obliged."

She stood back, looking at me critically while I stood there feeling like a wooden Indian in front of a cigar store. I said: "I got a piece of important business this evening. I believe I'll just wear this shirt. Kind of got a feeling it's a lucky shirt."

"You're going to see that Ruth woman, aren't you?"

"Yeah."

"Can I go?"

I shook my head. "No."

"But women can tell more about another woman than a man can."

I said: "Yeah, baby, but I'm looking at her as a possible member of the gang. And one outlaw can tell more about another outlaw than a citizen can. And you're still a citizen."

She went to her closet and started undressing. "I guess you talked to Wilcey."

"Oh, yes."

"How'd that go? Was it hard?"

"Oh, no harder than if I'd gone to ask him for the loan of his liver and lungs. I thought he was going to have apoplexy at first."

"But you talked him into it?"

"Not exactly talked him into it. More like forced him to see that what had to be done had to be done. He still likes it about as much as a *Meskin* likes snow."

We spent the balance of the afternoon talking and drinking and carrying on a little and then, about five o'clock, Wilcey knocked on the door. He stepped into the room just long enough to say hello to Marianne and then we went out. He looked drawn around the gills, but he hadn't changed his mind.

We went out the door of the hotel and turned left down the boardwalk. "Close enough to walk?" I asked him.

"Yeah," he said. "Not too far." He glanced around at me. "Where'd you get that shirt? I never seen you wear nothing that fancy before."

"Marianne gave it to me. Made me a present of it. It's silk."

"Hell you say!" he said, and I could see he was in about the same shape I'd been—never been given a present by a woman. He said, "Well, what caused her to do that? Is it some special day?"

"Said she just wanted to." Then, for meanness, I said, "Does it all the time. Don't Ruth give you little presents from time to time?" I glanced sideways at him. He was looking straight ahead, but I could see his face pink up a little.

He said, "Well, hell, it's all different for Ruth. She's an honest woman with an honest woman's debts. It's not like she was a whore with all that extra money laying around. Hell, I'm sure she's wanted to give me presents, but I ain't going to let her waste her money on me."

I wanted to laugh, but, instead, I said: "You know, Wilcey, I ain't paying a lot of attention about you keeping on calling Marianne a whore. That's what she is. You're a little tender right now, and I'm willing to let you get by with more than I ordinarily would. But you mark my words, the day is going to come when you'll regret what you've said about Marianne. In the end let's see who turns out to be the lady and who turns out to be the whore."

He said, sounding a little injured, "Hell, I never

meant nothing about Marianne being a whore. But facts is facts. Ruth is a lady and Marianne is a whore. Ain't no getting around that."

"We'll see," I said.

We walked on for several blocks and then turned south for about five more blocks. After one more turn Wilcey stopped in front of a little house about midway down the block. It was a little yellow painted frame house with a white picket fence around the yard. We stopped just outside the gate. Wilcey looked at me and said: "You sure this has got to be did?"

I nodded. "If you want to rob that transfer agent."

He swallowed and then looked at the house and then back at me. "I'm just going to take you in to meet her and then I'm going to leave. I ain't sure I'd be able to stand the look on her face when she finds out I'm an outlaw. I'll be waiting for you back at the Capital Saloon."

I half wanted to laugh at the look on his face. You'd of thought he was fixing to be hung. But I said, "What about her kids? They going to be running in and out?"

He shook his head. "Naw, they're gone. She shipped 'em off to her sister in Austin about ten days ago. Said it'd be better for them with her gone all day working."

Well, well, I thought. Seemed as though old Ruth was getting the decks all cleared for action. Hearing about her kids just made me all the more sure. I said to Wilcey, "I wouldn't worry about Ruth. You say her last name is Wilkenson?"

"Yeah."

We went on through the gate and then clumped up on the porch, our high-heeled boots making a pretty good racket. Wilcey opened the screen and knocked on the wooden door.

She opened the door immediately. She was small

and pretty and brown haired. She had on an ankle-length gray gown that was gathered at the throat with a clutch of lace.

She said, "My goodness, Denny, here you are. You and your friend come right in here."

Well, I'd never heard *Denny* before. So I said, "Yeah, Denny, go on in."

He looked around at me and blushed. Then he mumbled. "She just calls me that."

"My, my," I said. "I believe I like it."

We got inside and Wilcey give her a kind of awkward hug and then turned to me. He said, "This is the partner you've heard me talk about. This is—"

But he was so flustered I was afraid he'd give my right name. So I stepped forward, sweeping off my hat, and said, "Howdy, Mrs. Wilkenson, I'm Jim Wilson."

She dropped me a little curtsy and said, "Please call me Ruth, Jim. I feel as if I already know you. Now you gentlemen be seated and I'll get you some refreshments."

I looked at Wilcey and gave him a big grin, but he just turned his head, his face going beet red.

It was an ordinary enough looking sitting room. A morris chair and a stuffed divan with lace doilies on the arms. A few little tables and a rocking chair and a bunch of little knickknacks scattered all about. It was a woman's room all the way, and I had a quiet laugh to myself thinking of all the time Wilcey had spent over here and how often he'd probably knocked over one of them little dainty tables or broke one of them knickknacks or soiled one of them little doilies with his dirty hands. I bet he got his fair share of scolding.

Ruth came back in the room carrying a tray with a bottle of whiskey and two glasses on it. She set it down on a little table in front of the settee and said:

"This is some whiskey Denny brought over. I don't use it myself and I don't keep it in the house, but I don't hold against a man having a drink every now and again."

I said: "That's mighty kind of you, ma'am." I looked around at Wilcey. "But I didn't know that Wilcey had taken to drink. When did you start that, Denny?"

He said, "Aw, cut it out."

I picked up the bottle and poured me and Wilcey a pretty good slug. "Well," I said, taking up my glass, "here's luck all around." Then we knocked them straight back.

"My," Ruth said, "you certainly drink them right down."

"It's the toast," I said. "To luck. You won't get none, except bad, if you don't knock them straight back."

Wilcey suddenly got up. "I got to go," he said. "I'll be down at the saloon, Will."

Ruth said, "Why, Denny, wherever in the world are you going?"

"Will needs to talk to you. I'd just be in the way." He put on his hat and was out the door before either one of us could say another word.

"Well, whatever!" Ruth said, staring at the closing door. "What got into him?" She looked at me.

I shrugged and said, "Well, I kind of been wanting to talk to you, Ruth, and this seemed the best way."

"What could you have to talk to me about?"

"I'll get to that," I said. I got out a cigarillo and lit it and then realized I hadn't seen any ashtrays.

Ruth said, "Oh, you'll need a receptacle. Denny smokes those cigars too. Though I'll never understand why. They just smell awful to me." She got up and went out of the room. I could see me and her was just going to get along wonderfully well.

She brought me a little dinky thing back that I figured I could hit if I wasn't too drunk. But I never said nothing, just set it on the divan beside me.

Ruth sat down in a straight-backed chair opposite and put her hands on her knees. She said, "Now then?"

"Now then, what?"

"You wanted to talk to me."

"Oh, yeah." I leaned over and poured me another jigger of whiskey and then sat back on the divan, drawing on my cigarillo and looking at her. But if I expected I was going to make her nervous, I had another think coming. She just sat there, her hands on her knees, waiting for me to speak. I finally said, "You ain't from here, are you?"

"You mean, Houston? Oh, my, no."

"I mean Texas. You ain't from Texas."

For some reason that caused her to look a little uncertain. "Why do you ask that?"

"You don't sound like a Texan."

"Well, no." And she kind of hesitated. "Actually, I'm originally from Louisiana. New Orleans."

I said, "I thought so."

"Oh, really. Are you acquainted with that part of the country by chance?"

"Not so's you'd notice."

Then I sat for a good minute more, looking at her. Finally, I said, "I understand you and, uh, Denny are getting kind of serious."

She laughed. "Why, Jim, are you interested to see if I'm the kind of woman for your friend? Is that what this talk is to be about?"

I didn't flinch, just kept looking at her. "In a way," I said. "I'm looking out for him, if that's what you mean."

"Well," she said, "I don't quite know how I'm supposed to take that."

I said: "Well, according to Wilcey, you're such a lady that an old rough party like me might not know how to talk to you. Likely everything I say is going to be wrong. But I just got to plough ahead and let the devil take the hindmost."

She gave a little laugh. "My goodness, this sounds serious."

"Might be," I said.

We talked on, me just kind of nibbling around the edges, trying to get her to say something that would give me the opening to bring up the business of outlawry. But it was like trying to put a cat in a bucket of water. I never got so tired of hearing her southern "Oh, my!" and "My goodness!" and "Bless me!" in all my life. Finally, I said, "Ruth, you seem to be somewhat taken by Wilcey. And I know he sets great store by you. Ya'll thinking about tying the knot?"

"Well," she said, putting her hand to the lace at her throat, "the subject has come up. I'm sure Denny doesn't mind me talking about it to you, you and him being partners and all. But there are complications, Mr. Wilson. I'm afraid I have some burdens I wouldn't want to bring to Denny as a dowry."

"Yeah," I said dryly, "he told me. And that's kind of what I'm getting at."

"How is that, sir?"

I leaned forward. "Thing is, Wilcey needs some money, on account of you, and he needs it fast. See, we can't hang around Houston much longer."

"Any why not? Does your work call you elsewhere?"

I said: "Ruth, what do you really think Wilcey and I do for a living?"

"Why, just as he told me. You're in the cattle business."

I shook my head. "No, that's not the fact of the matter. Me and Wilcey are in the banking business."

"Well, now, why wouldn't Denny tell me that?"

I lit a cigarillo. "Probably because of the kind of banking business we're in. See, we mostly do withdrawals. Very seldom make deposits."

"How is that possible?"

I said, "With this," and whipped out my revolver and showed it to her.

She clutched at her throat and opened her mouth, but didn't say anything.

I watched her face closely. She was acting surprised, but she didn't *look* all that surprised.

Finally, she kind of stammered: "I still don't believe I understand you completely, sir."

I said, "Well, it's real simple. We're robbers. Mostly banks, but other things every now and again. We're bandits. Outlaws."

She stared into my face. "You're teasing me."

I shook my head. "No, and I think you already knew. Do we look like cattlemen?"

But she said, ignoring my remark that I thought she already knew, "Are you going to sit there and tell me my sweet, gentle Denny is a robber? An outlaw?"

I nodded. "As good as they come. He ain't the gun hand I am, but he's a good, steady man in any kind of a tight. We been doing business now for a number of years, and I can't say I've ever had a better partner."

She said, "I—I don't know what to think. You have caught me completely off guard, Mister Wilson."

She was playing it for all it was worth, putting a shaking hand to her throat and daubing at her mouth with a little dainty handkerchief.

I said, "Well, we figured you had to know, seeing as how you and Wilcey have been making plans. See, Wilcey is really a very honest man. That's why he wanted you to know. But he didn't have the courage to face you about it so that's why he asked me to do it. Now that ought to make you think considerable of Wilcey, him being willing to put his fate in your hands like that."

"What— Why his fate in my hands?"

It was fixing to be the payoff. It was showdown time. I said, "Well, we're wanted men. And if you was to tell on us Wilcey would either be killed or imprisioned."

"Oh, no!" she said quickly. "I could never do anything to hurt Denny. Oh, no, no, no! You may tell Denny to erase that worry from his mind. Oh, my." She began fanning herself with the little piece of handkerchief she had in her hand. "You have given me quite a turn, Mister Wilson, and I still don't know what to say."

I sat there watching her thoughtfully. She was taking big breaths, and I was watching her breasts strain against the material of her gown. She looked like she was pretty well built, though you really couldn't tell in the kind of gown she was wearing. I sat there idly wondering if Wilcey was able to get her to give up that genteel lady act when they went to bed. Likely she wouldn't even let him see her naked. It made me kind of half smile.

She said: "This has taken me so unawares! Denny and I were making plans. And now this! Oh, my! Oh, my!" Then she looked at the bottle of whiskey. "I wonder, Mister Wilson, if I might not have just a teeny bit of that spirit. Perhaps that would clear my head."

"Sure," I said. I poured her a good three inches in Wilcey's glass and got up and handed it to her. She took it with a hand that looked suspiciously steady for someone who'd had such a shock. Then, and even without benefit of the luck toast, she knocked that sucker straight back. She give a little gasp, but it

wasn't that much. I pretty well figured that lady had
had her share of the whiskey from time to time.

"Thank you, Mister Wilson," she said, handing me
the glass back. Then she commenced fanning herself
with that handkerchief. "It certainly warms a body,
don't it."

I said, "You want another one? If one helps, two is
twice as good."

"Well, maybe just a tiny bit more."

So I poured her another three fingers. This time
she only took half of it down in one swallow and then
sat there sipping at the rest.

She said, "I don't know what to do, what to think."

I sat back down and helped myself to the whiskey.
"Well, if you really care about Wilcey, ought not to
be hard to make up your mind. I can tell you what
Wilcey wants to do, what he's got in mind."

"Oh, yes, tell me that."

I drew on my cigarillo, watching her carefully
through the smoke. "He wants to marry you, wants to
marry you and quit the outlaw business. Take you off
somewhere where nobody would ever recognize him,
Colorado maybe or like that, and set up in the cattle
business as an honest man."

She put her hand to her mouth again. I swear the
damn woman ought to have taken to the stage. She
said, "Would it be possible? Could he really do it?"

I nodded. "Yes ma'am. You see, Wilcey ain't, by
nature, an outlaw. He just kind of drifted into it
through misfortune, and he's been looking for a way
out ever since. All he's been waiting for was to meet a
good woman, the kind of woman who'd be an inspira-
tion and give him the strength to lead a straight and
honest life. He thinks you're that woman, and now
that I've met you, I do too."

Hell, she wasn't the only one could playact.

"I'd give anything for that! I truly care for Denny.

Oh, my! Oh, my!"

I said, "Just one other little problem."

She looked at me fearfully.

I said: "Right now, Wilcey ain't got the money to finance an honest life. That's where you come in."

"Me? Why, Mister Wilson, I'm a poor widow. I have spoken of my burdens. I'm heavily in debt."

"Oh, I didn't mean you had any money. No, that's one of the reasons Denny is so set on getting some money. For you. To relieve your burdens so you two can get married and live an honest, Christian life."

"But how can I help?"

I said: "Well, there's a piece of business we can do that will give Wilcey the money he needs."

"Business?"

I took my cigarillo out of my mouth. "Robbery. We're thinking of doing a robbery."

"Oh!" She put her hand to her mouth again.

"Yes," I said. "Right here in Houston and right soon."

She just stared at me.

I said: "What do you think about that?"

"Well I—my goodness, Mister Wilson, I don't know what to think. This is all so new. It's coming so fast. My Denny—"

I said: "Well, you need to start getting used to it as fast as you can."

"Well, I'm trying. And I do so care about Denny."

I said: "That's good. Because we're going to need your help."

"My help? With what?"

Well, there it was. I said: "With the robbery."

Chapter Eight

The surprise this time was no playacting. It really took her off guard. She finally stammered out, "Me? Help with a robbery? Have you lost your senses, Mister Wilson?"

I shook my head slowly and drew on my cigarillo. "It's the only way, Ruth. The only way that we can do this business successfully so that you and Wilcey can go on and have that happy, honest life. I'm surprised you'd even hesitate. Not if you really care for Wilcey."

I watched her. I had a good idea what she was thinking. I figured her idea was to get Wilcey and me to rob that transfer agent, while she was an innocent bystander, and then to get the money off Wilcey. I reckoned she'd never figured on being a part of it.

She said, kind of nervously, "Well, of course I care for Denny. With all my heart. But this—Mister Wilson, are you seriously asking *me* to be part of a—a robbery!"

I nodded, enjoying myself. "Not a big part, ma'am. Just a real important part."

She straightened in her chair. "You're serious!"

"Yes, ma'am." I had debated before I come as to just how to play her, whether to force her to admit she'd known what we was all the way and that she'd been leading Wilcey toward the idea of robbing the transfer agent. But since I'd been talking with her, I'd seen that the direction to go was to give her the chance to "save a good man and return him to a life of honesty." That way I wouldn't be shoving her in a corner, and she could go with her playacting.

I said: "See, we're planning on holding up that transfer agent that brings down the money from the bank when ya'll send for it from the Cotton Exchange."

She didn't even bother to look surprised about that. Just kind of bit her lip and said, "I see."

I said, carefully, "I've heard from Wilcey that you've told him there's sometimes upward of fifty thousand in that satchel that agent carries."

She nodded, kind of dumbly. She was staring off in to space, like she wasn't even listening to me. Finally, she said, "I cannot believe Denny is allowing you to ask this of me."

I said, "Well, Ruth, it's for you. He wants to do it for you and him. He asked it of me as a favor, and, of course, Wilcey has done me so many favors through the years ain't much way I can refuse. On my part I studied this thing out from all angles, and the only way I can see to do it where we got a real good chance of success is with your help. It comes down to that. Do you want to help Wilcey get the money for you and his future or don't you? If it was up to me I'd just as soon ride on out of town and hang around the border for five or six months until a better job come along. I'd just as soon not do this one. But I done told Wilcey I would if we could get your help."

She sat there, biting her lip. "Oh, this is awful," she finally said. "I don't know what to think. It's such an audacious thing."

I nodded. "We're audacious robbers, ma'am."

"Would there—would I have to help much?"

She was weakening. I knew she would after she got over the shock of having me just put it up to her that we was robbers and was going to rob her place of business with her help. If I hadn't been sitting in front of her, I'd of bust out laughing at the surprise I'd give her. I said, just as serious as you please, "No, ma'am. You'd have such a little part I'm almost ashamed to mention it. You're back there in that cage and you know when they send for extra money and how much it is. All you got to do is give us the high sign. We'll work out the how of that later. But once we get the high sign that the money is coming we'll do the rest. That's all."

She looked around at me. "That's all? That's all I'd have to do?"

"Yes, ma'am. And then you and Wilcey will be on your way to that good, rich, honest life on a ranch somewhere in another state. Raising horses and cattle and children."

"I—well, I'd do anything to help Denny."

"Here's your chance."

"I don't know, Mister Wilson. I—I—I've never done anything like this before. You must know, I've led a sheltered life."

I bet she had. Probably had been a faro dealer in New Orleans. But the job was done. I could see that. All she wanted to do was playact for a while and convince me what a good woman she was.

I said: "Take a little more of this whiskey, Ruth. I know you don't hold with it, but this is a trying time."

"Yes, please."

I poured her out another hooker of whiskey, and she did a good job of nearly finishing it on the first pull. Probably if I wasn't there she wouldn't have bothered with the glass, just taken it straight out of the bottle.

I said, "Well, will you do it? Will you help yourself and your new husband?"

She clasped her hands together in her lap. She said, "Oh, I don't know, Mister Wilson! I work in the Cotton Exchange. Won't they suspect something? Denny has been seen there. We've been seen together."

"They'll never know it's Wilcey," I said. "They'll never recognize him."

"Will he be in disguise when you do your—your business?"

"We're always in disguise," I lied. "Now how about it?"

She said, "Oh, I can't think now. I can't give you an answer now. Please, you can understand that, Mister Wilson."

I shook my head. "No, that won't do, Ruth. See, I told you we're both wanted. We done been here too long now. If you won't go along with this, we're going to have to ride out of here tomorrow. All I promised Wilcey was I'd ask you and if you'd help then I'd do the job. But that if you wouldn't I was going to make some tracks."

"I don't know," she said. "I just don't know!" She was back to squeezing her hands together in her lap.

I got up and put on my hat. "Well, I'll have to leave now, Ruth. I take it you don't want to do it?"

"Oh, no!" she said. "No, no. I didn't say that. I just need to think." She got up and came over to me and put her hand on my shoulder. "Send Denny to me. Let me talk to him. Please."

I nodded. "All right. But I'll have to know in the morning."

I left after another minute or two, glad to get away from any more of her playacting. Walking back to town I had a pretty good laugh. She was a case, all right, and old Wilcey was swallowing it hook, line, and sinker. Well, for his sake I hoped I was wrong about her, hoped that maybe, under all that fooraw and foolishness, there might be a woman that would make Wilcey a good wife. God knows he deserved one.

I walked back to town toward a certain corner between the bank and the Cotton Exchange. I was studying out the route from there to Ruth's house in terms of the plan I had for the robbery. It seemed to be satisfactory for my purposes, but I wished it had been just a little farther.

I found Wilcey in the Capital Saloon. He was sitting at a table near the far wall, and he started up from his chair as soon as he saw me. I came up, dropped into a chair, and poured myself out a drink.

"Well, tell me! For God's sake!"

I took the time to take the shot of whiskey down. Wilcey was almost beside himself. It was the meanness coming out in me again, but I said, innocently, "Tell you what?"

He was about to explode. He said, violently, "Now, goddamnit, Will, don't play me. Tell me! How'd she take it?"

Considering all the hard times he'd given me about various females, I should have really drug it out and played him for all he was worth. But he looked so anguished and pitiful I didn't have the heart. I finally said, as sarcastically as I could manage, "You are to go to her. Them was almost her last words to me, 'Oh, send Denny to me!' So, Denny you'd best get along."

"But did you tell her? About what we do? Is it all right."

"Yes," I said.

Well, he looked that relieved I was almost sorry I'd told him so quick. Ain't often a man gets the opportunity to bring his fellow man such relief, and when

he does, he ought to savor it and not spend it frivo-
lously. He said, "Oh, my! Oh, my!"

Now here was a thing! The sonofabitch was starting to talk like her. If he picked up that habit, I'd
have him killed. I said: "And she's going to help us
with the robbery."

At that his eyes almost started out of their sockets.
"Are you sure, Will? Did she say she would?"

"Same as," I said. "She ain't come right out in so
many words, but if you work on her the right way she
will." I told him some of what we'd talked about,
ending with, "So she thinks the only way to make an
honest man of you is help you rob one more time."

I thought he was going to ask to shake my hand he
looked so grateful. He got up. "Guess I'd better hurry
along." He started to turn away and then swung back
to me. His face looked slightly troubled.

I said, "What's the matter now?"

He said, "I don't know. At first I was glad as hell
that Ruth would help us. Now I'm not so sure. You
reckon a real lady would do that?"

"Get out of here," I said. "Get out of here in a
hurry before I hit you with a chair."

He left and I walked back to the hotel. It was solid
dark and they'd lit them streetlights. I was mighty
impressed with a place that was so busy it had to
have the lights on *outside* at night.

Marianne was dressed and sitting in a chair reading
a dime novel when I come in. She looked mighty
pretty. I gave her a little kiss and then sat down on
the bed.

She put her book down. "Well? How did it go with
Wilcey's high-toned lady?"

I told her as much as I could, not being too chari-
table about the airs the lady put on or her playacting.

Marianne said, "So I take it the job is on?"

I nodded. "It don't look all that bad. Way I got it

figured I reckon we ought to be able to pull it off without too much risk to parties concerned and we ought to make a pretty fair payday."

Marianne was silent for a moment. Then she said, "I know you're the boss and you got to use your own best judgment, but I just hate to see you putting trust in that damn woman."

I shrugged. "Her part is so little ain't much she can do to foul us up. And I figure she knows which side her bread is buttered on. She wants Wilcey to have his pockets full when she finally takes him by the nose and leads him to the altar."

I went and cleaned up a little and shaved, and then me and Marianne went out to eat supper at Delmonico's. I was about oystered out so I ordered the spring chicken with cream potatoes and Marianne went for a steak. Waiting for the food to come, I said, "Well, I am going to hate to leave Houston on account of the grub. This past few weeks I've done got plumb spoiled, and it's going to be kind of hard to go back to beef and beans and what biscuits there are."

Marianne said, "Well, maybe you won't have to. I can cook, you know."

"The hell you say. When did you learn that?"

"What the hell you think we do in them whorehouses, send out for meals? Hell no, all them places got kitchens in them and the girls all do for themselves. In a way we're like a family. Fact of the matter is it's the only family most of us ever had. Or ever will have."

I said: "Seems like me and you both went running out the door at the same time. You to run off with a drummer, me to drift into the outlaw trade."

She said, "Maybe someday me and you can set up housekeeping somewheres. That way you won't have to make do with beef and beans. Maybe we could have a garden and a cow and some laying chickens and all like that."

I was busy with my food. But I did look up. "Sure, Marianne. Why not. Where? A thousand miles from here? I give up on that dream sometime back."

"Maybe it'll change. Maybe we could find a place."

"Sure," I said. "Be the easiest thing in the world. That is if it wasn't for sheriffs and marshals and the other law that is mighty interested in my whereabouts."

She put her fork down. "Will, what are we going to do? You and me?"

"I don't know what you mean."

"Yes you do."

"All right, I do. One thing we ain't going to do about it is to talk of it right now. Right now I got my mind on that robbery and making a safe getaway. After that we may talk. Or after that I may be dead. But right now is not the time to worry about it."

It kind of put a damper on the conversation.

I had finished eating and was drinking a cup of coffee when two men come in the café. It is my custom just kind of automatically to check everybody out that comes into a room where I'm sitting. I wasn't paying much attention to the first man, didn't know him, and I couldn't quite see the second man, not until they went around a table and kind of squared up toward us. The man in the back was middle-aged, a little gone to flesh, and I'd seen him some years back in Corpus Christi. He might have changed some, but the badge on his shirt hadn't.

I leaned forward, kind of shielding my face with my hand. I said, "I got to get out of here. I'm going to get up and walk out just like I was stepping out on the street for a newspaper. Let a little time pass and then pay the check. I'll be up in the room."

Good woman that she was she never said a word,

just nodded and went on eating. I got up very casually and then, being careful to keep my back to the table the lawman had taken, walked on out the door and headed straight for the hotel. It was bad luck, that face from my past, but I'm sure he'd of figured it was very good luck, considering the amount of reward that was probably on my head, if he'd seen me. Wasn't the slightest doubt in my mind, but what he'd of known me on sight.

I got up in the room and put a chair against the door, sat down on the bed and loosened my revolver in its holster. It had give me a bad start and no mistake. It was also a warning to me. We'd been in Houston so long with nothing happening that I'd got to feeling that wasn't nothing going to happen, that nobody would recognize me, that maybe the law had even forgotten all about me.

Well, that kind of thinking can get you killed.

No, it was becoming clear now that we'd been in one spot too long and the quicker we could pull that robbery and get out of town the safer it was going to be. Sitting there, I resolved on the spot to quit making myself so obvious in public. I was getting careless.

Marianne tried the door and I had to get up and let her in. She took off her shawl and said: "What was it?"

"Lawman. From Corpus Christi where I used to run. A lucky thing I seen him before he seen me."

"Is it like this often?"

"Yeah," I said. "Very often." I sat down and pulled off my boots. "Let's go to bed. I'm tired."

Next morning I went down to the telegraph office and sent Chulo a wire to come at once. I wasn't worried about him coming. He'd arrive unless he was dead or in jail.

Marianne was out when I got back and I was glad. I wanted some time to think. I pulled a chair up in front of the window, turned it backward so I could straddle it, got me a drink of brandy, lit a cigarillo, and then sat there staring out and trying to get all the ins and outs of the robbery straight in my mind.

I don't know how long I thought, but the level had gone down in the bottle pretty good before I was satisfied. Some of the details were still not to my liking, but they'd just have to shove themselves into place. The plan was as good as I could come up with, all things considered, and I figured it had a better-than-average chance of succeeding.

I went out of the hotel and ran into Marianne on the street. "Where you been?" I asked her.

"Just looking the town over. I'm getting like you, I'm about ready to move on."

"You mean now?"

She gave me a sharp look. "Can't you keep anything in your head five minutes? I mean afterward."

We walked a ways down the street and found a little café and had the noon meal. I didn't figure to be going back into Delmonico's anymore. I was also going to change my hotel.

While we were eating, I told Marianne what her part would be in the robbery. It never fazed her. She just shrugged and said, "Is that all? You mean I don't even get to use a gun?"

"No, but I got something for you to do that you ain't going to like all that well."

"And what's that?"

"Just as quick as I can get it arranged I'm going to move you over to Ruth's house. You'll be there until after the robbery."

She bridled instantly. "The hell I will!"

I shook my head patiently, expecting her reaction to be what it was. "You got to, baby. The only way." I went ahead and explained to her that she couldn't stay with me else, in case I was recognized during the robbery, she would be identified with me and that would ruin everything. "And I can't just put you in another hotel. This town's going to be hot as a pistol after we pull that job, and you'll have to be here for at least two more days. No, I got to have you somewhere completely out of sight. Besides, I want you to keep an eye on Ruth. See, you don't know what the rest of the plan is, but just trust me it's important you stay over at Ruth's."

Well, she put up a little more squawk, but, good and sensible girl that she was, she finally subsided and give in. But she said, "How are you and I going to be together?"

"Very little, until this thing is done."

"Hell, Will," she said, "I didn't come here to enjoy the company of a woman. Especially *that* kind of woman."

"There's no help for it. From now until that robbery is done we've all got to be mighty careful."

"When do you figure?"

"As soon as Chulo gets here as we can do it. If he was here now I'd pull it tomorrow."

I saw Wilcey that afternoon and told him about Marianne moving in with Ruth. He tried to put up a squawk also, but I nailed him in his tracks. I'd had just about enough of him and that damn woman. I said, "Listen, Wilcey, you say another goddamn word about that great lady of yours and that Marianne is just a whore and I'm going to pack my traps and get the hell out of Houston and you can get along on your own. From now on you do what I tell you without a whimper. I know you're so wrapped up in that gown tail that you can't think, but you better begin to thinking, or at least you better keep your mouth shut around me."

He didn't like it, but he took it. I imagine he figured he didn't have no choice. I know a woman changes a man, and I knew that he'd eventually come back some nearer to the old Wilcey, but for the time being he was a pain in the ass. Then I told him I wanted him to move out of the hotel. "I'm going to, as quick as I get Marianne over to Ruth's. And you've got to do the same. Find you a little out of the way place and be sure and don't call attention to yourself. Also, I want you to buy you a suit of clothes."

He looked baffled. "A suit of clothes?"

"Yeah, like these dandies around here wear. A sack suit, or whatever they call it. One of them kinds got a vest underneath."

"Whatever for?"

My patience was near gone with him. I said, "Just do it, goddamnit. You'll know the why of it soon enough. Just buy the goddamn suit and secret it in your room. I'll tell you when to put it on."

That night we got Marianne over to Ruth's. We let her go in first and then Wilcey and I slipped in one at a time. I had told Marianne to have the lamps turned down and the shades pulled so that we wouldn't be so visible from the street. Wilcey thought it was unnecessary precautions, but I didn't agree. "You can't be too careful in this business," I told him. One thing I liked about Ruth's house was that it wasn't nearby to anything. The next house was a good fifty yards away, and there was nothing behind her except a few acres of open fields. That meant there'd be little chance of Marianne being noticed as an occupant of the house.

When Wilcey and I got inside, I got everybody to sit down. Ruth wanted to make a to do about getting some "refreshments" like we were having a party, but I got it quick through to her that from here on out it was going to be all business.

I said: "Now I can't tell anybody anything, just yet.

I won't know the when of this thing until Chulo gets here."

Ruth said, "My, who's Chulo?"

I give her a hard look. With the lamps down low the room was dim and flickering. I said, "Ruth, one thing you'll come to learn about this business is to not ask any questions. What you'll need to know you'll find out soon enough."

She and Wilcey were sitting on the divan together. He had his arm up along the top of the backrest, not quite around her shoulders. I was sitting in a chair opposite them, and Marianne was in the morris chair to my left. I said: "Wilcey and I are going to be leaving in just a minute and we won't be seeing much of ya'll. When Chulo gets here, we'll have one more meeting, then, if we're lucky, we'll pull the job that next day."

Wilcey said: "What the hell are you talking about, Will? You mean I ain't going to be able to come over and see Ruth?"

I shook my head. "No, you ain't."

He said, "Aw, hell!"

I said, "Listen, Wilcey, it's important none of us be seen together from this point onward. I've asked Marianne to stay in the house until the robbery and she's said she'd do it." I looked over at her. "Isn't that right, babe?"

She nodded. "Yes."

"Now she ain't going to want to do that. But I don't want none of the neighbors connecting her to this house. It's a long shot, I agree, but they ain't no point in taking chances. The women will stay on here for a couple of days after we're gone, and I don't want no connection made between them and us. You got that?"

"I guess," he said reluctantly.

Ruth was fanning herself with a newspaper. She

seemed to be eternally fanning herself with something. She clutched at Wilcey's arm, and said, "Oh, my, I'm just terrified."

I looked at Marianne and she raised her eyes to the heavens. Then I got up. "Well, that's about it. Marianne ain't going to show herself out of here except at night and, Ruth, you just go ahead as you've been going. Don't do nothing out of the ordinary. When Chulo gets here, we'll have one last meeting and then we'll do the deed. Marianne, if either of you have to get in touch with us, Ruth should leave a message at the Texan café about breakfast time. That's where I'll be taking my meals. If it's a big emergency, come to my hotel, the Prairie Hotel."

I give Marianne a brief little kiss and told her I'd see her in just a few days. "It'll be over quick," I said. I whispered in her ear, "Get along as best you can with Ruth. And keep an eye on her."

Then Wilcey and I were back out in the street, walking through the dark night toward town. He said, "I wish you wouldn't have talked so hard to Ruth. She ain't used to it."

I just said, "Aw, shut up, Wilcey."

Chulo showed up two days later. Since I'd known I'd be checking out of my hotel, I'd sent word he was to watch for me in the Capital Saloon, since I had the habit of dropping around there two or three times a day. Sure enough, I walked in there one morning, and there was that mean *Meskin* sitting at a table over against the wall, looking just as evil as ever. I walked over, kicked me a chair out, and said, "Hello, Nigger!"

He smiled big, them white teeth flashing in that black face of his. *"Qué pasa, amigo!"*

He clapped me on the shoulder and damn near broke it. I tell you, he was one big, mean, strong *Meskin.* I planned to be eternally grateful he was my

friend and not my enemy. I took a good look at him
before I answered. He had a little furrow on the side
of his neck, still a little inflamed, that looked to be
where a bullet had cut its near course to his vitals. I
said, "The hell with what's been happening with me.
Where the hell did you get the little souvenir in your
neck?"

"Aaah," he said. "That. Is no *importa*."

"Tell me all the same," I said.

He shrugged. "They have the new lawman in San
Antone. He does not understand from the old law
that you don't make trouble for Chulo if he is no
cause trouble in San Antone. So I shoot hem."

"You kill him?"

"He got pretty dead. That what took me so long.
The other law tell me I got to get out of town for a
leettle. Until it cool off. *Sabe?* So I am hiding out. My
cousin have to find me. That what take so long after
you send for me for me to get here."

All that meant was that he'd rode 140 miles in just
a little better than two days. Oh, no, old Chulo wasn't
a damn bit dependable. Not much more dependable
than death or the dawn.

I said, though, "Well, you taken your old goddamn
sweet time getting here. And me with a big job
planned. But I'm going to let it go this time. But only
because I feel sorry for you."

He grinned big at that and clapped me on the
shoulder again. I could do without them friendly taps
of his. He said, "*Mi amigo*, Weelson! It is very good
for Chulo that Weelson is *mi amigo*!"

"Yeah," I said, and thought: And it's damn good for
"Weelson" that the Nigger is his *amigo*.

He said: "What we do, Weelson? We make plenty
money?"

"Hell yes, you ignorant *Meskin*. Of course we make

plenty money. What the hell you think we rob for? Of course to make plenty money."

We drank a little longer and then paid the score, and I led him back to my hotel, after bading him to walk a sufficient distance behind me and to not let on that he knew me. We walked into the lobby and I asked for my key in a loud voice so Chulo'd know the number, then I left him downstairs and went on up to my room. Of course this little hotel was nothing like what I'd moved out of. They didn't have a bathroom on every floor. In fact, they done damn good to have one at all. For the entire place.

I got to my room with its little narrow bed and its chipped water pitcher and sat down to await Chulo's coming. I never thought to wonder if they'd have a room vacant that he could take. I just went ahead and guessed such a little second-rate outfit wouldn't be all booked up. But as time passed, I commenced to worry. Then there came a knock on the door and I took the chair away and let him in.

"Where the hell you been, Nigger?"

He give me a kind of misunderstanding look. "I got to get the gear for this *Meskin* from the stable to take to my room. I do et wrong?"

Well, I had to laugh. I said, "No, you dumb son-ofabitch. Get in here."

He'd gotten him a room in the hotel all right and was otherwise fixed up.

We got settled and had us a drink out of the bottle I had there, and I told him as much as I could about the job. Of course, I'd never had to tell Chulo much about any job. All he cared about was that I was calling the shots and that everything would work out for the best. Sometimes his faith in me was just a little more than a body could bear.

But I strained it. I got him up where he could look out the window and I said, "You see that gent down there in that suit? Well, tomorrow, early, I want you to go and buy you one just like it. It don't have to be first-class goods, but I want you looking some different than you do now."

Well, he couldn't believe it. But I went on convincing him until he did. He said he didn't know where he'd get such a thing, but I told him to keep on walking up and down Main Street until he run into the place he could.

Then I said: "You well mounted? Did you buy you a good horse in San Antonio?"

"Of course. Just as you told me."

After that I told him to keep himself close, for I didn't know at what minute I'd want him. "And, remember, we can't be seen much together. If I can find Wilcey we'll all take a ride out in the country to a ranch ya'll need to know where is."

I located Wilcey a little after noon in a café by the hotel. I made a signal and he joined me outside. I said, "About one thirty get your horse and meet me and Chulo on the southwest edge of town. There's a little road goes to Roan's Prairie, if you can find it."

He said: "The *Meskin* here?"

"Yeah."

"How's he doing?"

"He managed to kill a tenderfoot lawman in San Antonio. But, other than that, he's fine. Broke as usual. Says he spent all his money on 'the weemens' in San Antonio."

We parted and I went to another café and had my noon meal. After that I got my horse and rode out east of town, taking a route that threw me very near Ruth's house, the route we'd be taking after the robbery. I was looking for a place a little way out of town to hide the horses. I found it a couple of miles out of town. It was near perfect, a little sinkhole surrounded by a grove of stunted post oak trees. Except for town and a few remote farmhouses, there wasn't a thing for miles. We could hide the horses there, make the switch from the buggy, and have an excellent chance of not being seen at all.

I rode on back to town, found Chulo at the hotel, and told him to get his horse and follow me out of town at a distance.

Wilcey was waiting just where the road forked off to go to Roan's Prairie. He and Chulo give each other a big hello and a little hoorahing and then we set off for old man Drake's. Wilcey wanted to know where we were going, and I said, "A ranch we'll probably be hiding out on for a couple of days after the robbery. Sort of let things settle down. But I want to warn you that this old man who owns the place is mighty peculiar and mighty persnickety. Don't do nothing to get his ire up."

Soon we'd raised the place out of the prairie, made our howdys, and then we were sitting in the parlor with old man Drake. I said, "Well, here's my two *amigos* will be resting up on your place if it's still all right."

But he was staring at Chulo with his sharp, old eyes. He said, "That's about the meanest-looking goddamn *Meskin* I ever seen. Does he mind you?"

"Yeah, he minds me. Don't you, Chulo?"

The Nigger grinned big, them white teeth flashing in that black face. "For sure. *El Senor es el jefe.*"

"I'm glad he recognizes you as the boss. I'd hate for that sonofabitch to get on a tear."

"No, he's halter broke. He's all right."

Drake's son, Amos, was there, a big coltish boy in his mid-twenties. By that age most boys have become men, but I could look in his face and eyes and tell he wasn't ever going to become a man, no matter how many years he lived. He reminded me of Tod, that

old partner of mine who'd been about the biggest
fool of any man I'd ever known.

He proved what a fool he was just a little bit later.
We'd been sitting there, talking to his daddy, and
he'd been leaned up against the wall watching us.
Then, without the slightest bit of a how-do-you-do, he
walks up to me and sticks out his hand and says, "Let
me take your pistol for a minute. I want to look at
it."

Well, I was that astounded. You got to be awful
good friends with a man to make such a request, and
I'd never even seen this boy before. I looked at him
and then I looked at his daddy. Finally, I said, "Well,
I don't reckon."

Fortunately his daddy said, "Amos, get the hell
away from that gentleman." He was furious. He said,
"That ain't good manners, boy! What the hell's the
matter with you."

But he never left the room. Anybody with any
sense would have been so shamed he'd of absented
himself. But not that boy. He just went back and
lounged against the wall, watching us.

I said, "Well, Drake, is it a deal? Can we depend
on your place when we need it?"

He said, "When you figuring?"

I just had to shrug. I said, "Today's Tuesday. I figure either Thursday or Friday. That's as close as I
can make it."

He said: "That's all right with me."

I asked him, "You still won't set a price?"

He said, "Let's see how you boys do."

"But you guarantee us safety here?"

"Best I can figure it. Hell, I ain't going to rob you.
If you make a pretty good payday and they's a little
something spilling over, I'll take it. Why shouldn't
I?"

I said, "All right. You got a deal. Look for us when you see us come riding up. And you'll answer for your son and your hired hands?"

"Goddamnit, don't you question my word! Anybody that's here is for the place."

So we left it at that and rode away.

On the way back in to town Wilcey said, kind of anxiously, "You say we're going to hole up there after the robbery. I don't mind the old man, but that son ain't too much to my liking."

I was feeling the same way, but I said, "It ain't the son running the place. It's the old man. And we got his word on it. That's all I can tell you. Now, let it alone."

To tell the truth, I was in a little bit of a growling mood myself. Marianne had been gone for a little better than two days, and I was missing the hell out of her. Of course, I wasn't going to admit it to nobody, but that was the fact of the matter.

Next morning I saw to it that we all bought our suits, and then I led Wilcey and Chulo out and showed them where we were going to hide the horses.

I said, "Wilcey, as soon as we get back to town I want you to rent a buckboard from a livery. Get it for a week so you can take it in and out whenever you want."

He said, "I guess you ain't going to tell me what we need a buckboard for?"

"I will tonight," I said. "We're going to all gather up at Ruth's, and I'm going to tell you the plan I got figured out."

I had me some supper just before dark and then sat in my room until I judged it was time to go. Then I knocked on Chulo's door. He come out, as I'd told him to do, and followed me on foot to Ruth's house.

Wilcey was already there. Me and Marianne give

each other a brief kiss and hug, but we didn't make no show out of it like Wilcey was doing with Ruth.

Chulo turned out to be a hit with the women. Ruth said, just as if Chulo wasn't there, "Now I feel as if this is really a robbery. You and Denny look like gentlemen, but he looks like what I'd imagined a real brigand would appear as."

But Chulo was more taken with Marianne than anything. He kept trying to get near her and he kept saying, "Such a pretty weemen!"

Until I made it clear to him. "Listen, Nigger, this woman belongs to me. You look, but you don't touch."

Marianne said, "Let him go on talking. Hell, a woman likes to hear that kind of stuff."

I told her dryly, "Don't get to feeling too big about it. If you ain't got a peg leg and a harelip, Chulo is going to fall in love with you. He likes 'weemen.' Of all shapes and sizes."

There was a little bit of a kind of celebration to the gathering, caused, I supposed, by the fact that me and Wilcey hadn't seen our women in a few days.

But I got them settled down. And once I went over the plan for the robbery, and what each person's part would be, there wasn't a smile in the lot.

Wilcey said, kind of nervously, "Will, this seems awful risky to me. I mean, right there in broad daylight."

I said, "Well, then why don't you march yourself down to that bank tomorrow and get them to transfer the money in the dark of night down some alley."

Of course he didn't have much to say to that.

Marianne said: "Hell, I thought it was a robbery. Ain't it supposed to be kind of unsafe?"

I was grateful to her for that. I said, "So anybody that wants to back out better do it right now." I looked straight at Ruth. "Else we're going to do it like we planned. And anybody that don't hold up to their end is likely to get us all killed."

But she never made no sign, other than to look down at her hands in her lap.

I got up. "We're going to slip on out of here. Wilcey, you're to get that buckboard at the crack of dawn tomorrow morning. Tie your horse on behind it. Chulo and I will follow you out to where we're to hide the horses. We'll leave them there and ride back into town with you on the buckboard. And don't forget to get you a few sacks of feed to carry around so it'll look like you've got legitimate business."

Just before we left I took Marianne aside. "How you holding up?"

She hit me in the chest with her little fist. She said, "If I'd known I was going to have to spend time with that bullshit broad, I'd of never come to see you."

"Just a little more time. What do you think of her?"

"I think she's phony as a three-dollar bill. You let Wilcey marry her and you damn sure ain't no friend of his."

I said, "But will she go through with her end of the robbery?"

She pulled her head back and looked at me. "Are you kidding? If ya'll don't do it, I figure she'll try to bring it off on her own. Hell, you ain't planned this job. She has."

I said, "That's what I figured."

Then I kissed her. I said, "I won't see you again until I'm putting a gun to your head and forcing you into a wagon. Don't forget I kind of got tender thoughts of you."

She got real close to me and put her arms around my back. She said, "Ain't but one gun I want you putting close to my head and it ain't the one you carry in that holster by your side."

We left. I told them, "I just hope it happens tomorrow."

Chapter Nine

〜〜〜〜〜〜〜〜〜〜〜〜〜〜〜〜〜〜〜〜〜〜〜〜〜〜〜〜〜

Next morning, early, me and Chulo followed Wilcey out to the spot I'd selected to hide the horses and tied them in the oak grove with loosened cinches. Then we rode back to town with Wilcey on the buckboard. He let us out well below town and me and Chulo, keeping separate, walked on back to the hotel. I went up to my room and put my sack suit on over my regular clothes. I'd bought it a size too large, but it was still mighty cumbersome to be wearing two suits of clothes.

I knocked on Chulo's door after I was ready. I said, "Let's go."

Well, if you think I was a revelation in my city suit of clothes, you ought to have seen Chulo. I'm sure he'd bought the biggest size they had, but as it was, his shoulders was near about to split the cloth of the coat. I never said anything to him, but if you've ever seen a pig wearing a dress for the dance, he looked just about as much at home in that suit as a pig would.

We got on downstairs and then went and took up the positions I'd laid out for us the night before. I taken my station up right across from the Cotton Exchange. Chulo was down from me about ten yards.

Wilcey, sitting on the seat of his buckboard, was right across the street.

All we were waiting for was for Ruth to walk to the door of the Cotton Exchange and give us the signal that the money had been sent for by fanning herself with her handkerchief. Her job, once she heard her boss say they needed some more money, was to get faint, ask to get some fresh air, and then walk to the door and signal us. That was all the job she had in the matter. That and to take care of the money once we got it to her house.

I wasn't too hopeful in the morning. She'd already told me that it wasn't until afternoon that they generally had to have the extra money. But I wanted to be ready, in any case.

But the morning came and went without a signal. About noon I let Wilcey and Chulo know that it was all right to go and eat. Wilcey come into the same little café I was eating at, and even though he didn't sit down with me, he muttered as he passed my table, "I can't keep sitting there like I ain't got no business in town. Somebody is sure to notice me."

I calculated my time to leave as he did. I said, "You're setting in front of a general mercantile. Go sit on that bench and act like you're waiting for somebody."

This was done out on the boardwalk in passing. I went on back to my station and he went back to his. I was pleased to note, however, that he quit sitting in the buckboard with the reins in his hands and, instead, took him a seat on the bench that stood in front of the mercantile store. I knew his brains were addled out of looove, but he didn't have to keep on proving it.

Lord, it was hot that afternoon, wearing them two suits of clothes. I hadn't had a tie on since I could remember last, and I kept clawing at it and that buttoned shirt collar and just squirming around in all that heat.

Two o'clock came and went and then three and then four. And then the Exchange closed without them sending for a damn dollar.

I figured my partners would understand, so I just quit my station and wandered on back to my hotel. First thing I did when I got in my room was to shed that goddamn suit. It was black and hot as hell and made me feel like an undertaker, a profession I ain't a damn bit interested in finding out more about.

Just as I'd figured, they showed up at the door, Wilcey first and then Chulo. I let them in. I said, "Goddamnit, we ain't supposed to be seen together."

Wilcey said, "Hell, Will, what do you reckon I'm made out of, stump wood? I sat over there with my heart in my mouth half hoping it would come and half hoping it wouldn't. You realize we're fixing to rob something like fifty thousand dollars in the broad goddamn daylight in downtown Houston! Damn!"

I said: "It ain't going to be no tougher than when we robbed that ranch in the Panhandle. Easier, maybe."

"This scares the hell out of me, Will."

I looked at the Nigger. "It scare you, Chumacho?"

He give me that big grin. "No, no is afraid. I don't like them clothes you make me wear."

"Neither do I," I said. "But it's necessary."

Wilcey said, "Now what do we do?"

"We try again tomorrow. What the hell you think?"

"Well, what if they don't send for money tomorrow?"

I said, "Hell, Wilcey, I don't know. I guess we try again Monday."

"We keep walking around in these monkey suits, and we're pretty soon going to draw some attention.

And how much longer can I keep on parking that
buckboard on the street?"

"People are paying you a hell of a lot less attention
than you think they are."

Then he said, "I'm going to go see Ruth tonight."

"No, you're not. You're staying the hell away from
there. I've got to go over and make sure nothing went
wrong today and make sure the women still know
they're to do the same thing tomorrow. So I don't
want two of us around there."

He said, "Hell, you're just going to see Marianne."

I said, "Now cut that out, Wilcey. We pull this job
off you'll get to see Ruth the rest of your life."

"Hell, Will, I can slip in there without nobody
seeing me."

"I said no, now leave it at that. And you better not
slip over there thinking I won't know."

I went over a couple of hours after it was dark,
slipping in through the back door. Ruth and Marianne were sitting in the parlor. I said, "Well, ladies,
we didn't do no business today."

Ruth said, "I don't know if I'm not just that glad
that we didn't. Mister Wilson, it seems so *dangerous*.
I'm just mighty afraid something bad is going to happen."

I said to Marianne, "Did you get tired of waiting?"

"Yes. I never thought nothing was going to happen."

I'd had her just up the street from the Cotton Exchange, shopping around in stores and sitting in
cafés, all with her eye to me and the signal I'd give
once I received one from Ruth.

I said, "Ya'll both still feel all right? I mean, you
understand we're going to be trying it tomorrow." I
said it to both of them, but I was asking only about
Ruth.

She said, "I just don't know, Mister Wilson. I'm

getting more and more afraid all the time. Today I thought if they were to send for money that my heart would just stop."

Marianne was sitting behind her and she just rolled her eyes toward the ceiling. I said, "Listen, Ruth, it's too late to get cold feet now. You better get a little courage from somewhere. Out of the bottle if necessary."

Marianne walked out with me. She said, "If I have to spend twenty-four more hours with that damn silly woman I'm going to go crazy. This thing had better come off tomorrow."

I kissed her. "It will. You feel all right, other than staying with Ruth?"

She hit me on the chest with her little fist. "Goddamnit, I didn't come to Houston to sleep by myself. You sonofabitch."

I said, "How the hell you think I feel? But it has to be. Now you get old Ruth's courage bolstered up."

She said, "Hell, that damn woman don't need her courage boosted. She's damn near already got the money counted."

I walked back to the hotel in a very thoughtful mood. I'd never pulled a robbery with two women before, and I didn't quite know how to handle it. I'd had good experience at running a gang, such as Chulo and Wilcey, but handling women was a new deal for me.

I got up next morning with that feeling I always get when I'm going to pull a job. There may be those who don't get all tensed up and dry mouthed, but I ain't one of them. I'm all right once the job starts, but the waiting and the anticipation are sometimes near more than I can stand.

We took up our stations about an hour before noon—me and Chulo down the street toward the bank, but still close enough to the Cotton Exchange that I could see Ruth if she come to the door, Marianne across the street in a little café with a seat by the window, and Wilcey back at his station by the mercantile store. I knew we was going to get conspicuous pretty soon, but there wasn't any help for it.

Noon came and went. We all went to eat and then came back. Then it was two o'clock and I was beginning to think nothing was going to happen. I'd just got out a cigarillo to light it and really wasn't watching the door of the Cotton Exchange that close, but in that instant I caught the sight of something out of the corner of my eye. It was Ruth standing in the door fanning herself with her handkerchief.

Well, my heart jumped into my throat, but there was nothing for it but to go ahead with the robbery. I raised my hat, which was the signal to Wilcey and Marianne. I waited long enough to see that they'd gotten it, and then Chulo and I turned and started walking down the street toward the bank. Glancing across the street, I could see that Marianne had gotten up out of her seat in the café and was coming outside and that Wilcey had left his bench and was climbing into the buckboard.

Chulo and I walked on up until we were nearly opposite the bank. We took a station a little above the bank and just sort of leaned up against a building side, acting like we were just talking and smoking.

Well, I don't know how much time passed, but if Christmas had ever been slower than the time it took them transfer agents to come out of that bank, there wouldn't have been a schoolboy alive today.

But they finally come out, the two guards on the outside marching along with their shotguns held up across their chests, and the middle man, the man with the pouch, carrying his with one hand, using the other to hold on to the money bag.

Chulo and I crossed the street and fell in behind

them, walking about ten yards back, at first, but intending on catching up in a hurry when the time came.

It wasn't a real complicated plan, but it did count on some mighty close timing. We were a block from where I intended it to happen. Looking up the street I could see Marianne out on the sidewalk, starting toward us. Wilcey was just waiting with the buckboard, a few yards down from the corner where I intended for the robbery to take place.

We walked that block, people all around us, while I thought about all the things that could go wrong. I tell you, at that point it seemed so risky I damn near felt like calling it off. But I glanced over at Chulo and he was just walking along, looking as contented as a puppy with a new bone.

Hell with it, I thought. It's worth the chance.

Those guards hadn't even glanced back at us. I quickened my pace as we got nearer the end of the block. Marianne was already starting across the street to meet us, and I could see Wilcey pulling his buggy out in the street, getting ready to swing around the corner.

Then it all began to happen. Marianne had timed herself just as perfectly as you could ask. She stepped up on the boardwalk just as the guards were about five yards from the end of the block. She got to them and dropped her purse right at their feet. She said, "Oh," and put her hand to her mouth.

The two with the shotguns, as I'd figured, both leaned over to retrieve her purse for her. As they did Chulo and I suddenly surged forward, drawing our pistols as we did. Almost together we each clubbed one of the guards over the head. They dropped like they'd been poleaxed. Then, before he could even think what was happening, I'd jerked the shotgun out of the hands of the guard with the money and Chulo had collared him around the neck. Then I grabbed Marianne, trying to look like I was handling her roughly, but trying not to hurt her. As I hustled Marianne into the street and Chulo half drug the guard, Wilcey come wheeling around the corner with the buckboard, skidding to a stop. In less time than it takes to tell it, Chulo had thrown the guard in the bed of the wagon and I'd shoved Marianne in. Then Chulo and I climbed in. The first thing Chulo did, even as Wilcey was whipping the buckboard horse into a gallop, was to knock the guard out we had in the buckboard. He keeled over with a sigh. Sitting in the back of the buckboard, I jerked out my pistol to cover our retreat.

There wasn't a shot fired.

There were plenty of people on the boardwalk, but they were just staring after us like they'd never seen anything like it in their lives.

Which was what I'd counted on. But, for insurance, I'd made it seem like we were capturing Marianne, and I damn sure didn't figure anyone would fire a shot after us with a woman in the buckboard.

Once we were moving, Chulo went to work with a hacksaw we'd brought along, cutting the chain between the money pouch and the guard's wrist. As soon as that was done, I handed it to Marianne and she lifted her skirts and petticoats and attached it between her legs with some cloth strips she'd tied there.

We were racing down the street, Wilcey whipping the hell out of the horse, the houses flying by. I figured we had a good ten to fifteen minutes before any pursuit could develop. I leaned over next to Marianne. "You all right, sweetheart?"

She give me a little smile. "Never been shoved around like you did me."

"I didn't hurt you?"

She laughed. "No, it's fun."

By then she had that money pouch tucked up between her legs and her skirts smoothed down so you couldn't have told she had it even if she'd been standing next to you.

Wilcey took us flying around a corner, turning onto Ruth's street. I looked over at the guard; he was still unconscious.

Then we were coming to a skidding stop about fifty yards from Ruth's house. Marianne and I made a little show, in case anyone was watching, of her escaping from the buckboard with me trying to stop her. She wouldn't go directly to Ruth's house, but would, instead, circle around and approach it from the back.

But as soon as she was gone, I leaped back in the buckboard and we tore out up the street, heading for the road where we had the horses tied.

The guard was still out. Chulo was grinning. Hell, it had gone smoother that I'd hoped. But, by damn, it had been a pretty good plan—in spite of all the misgivings Ruth and Wilcey had felt.

We turned onto the road out of town, and as soon as we'd left the last of the houses behind, Wilcey pulled up the buckboard and I rolled the guard out the back and onto the ground. He looked awful limp and I hoped Chulo hadn't hit him hard enough to kill him, but there was no time to worry about that, for we were tearing down the road again.

In a few minutes we were at the little grove where we'd tied the horses. We leaped out. Wilcey had loose tied the reins to the whip socket, and he give that buckboard horse a slap across the behind with his hat that sent him tearing on up the road. Then we run for our horses, jerking off them suits as we did, getting down to our natural clothes. We didn't say a word to each other until we'd stuffed those suits in our saddlebags, mounted up, and I was leading us off toward the southwest, taking off across the open plains at a pretty good clip.

Finally, I pulled us down to a walk. Wilcey was on my left and Chulo to my right. Wilcey looked at me and said, "That's the goddamnedest thing I've ever seen." He stared at me a minute longer. "I still don't believe it went off that slick."

I said, "It ain't over yet."

"Hell, Will, it's pie all the way from here. I got to hand it to you."

I said: "Damnit, don't put your mouth on our luck. Leave it alone."

We rode a little farther and then I pulled us to a stop. I said, "All right, here's where we split up. Everybody know how to find old man Drake's place?"

They nodded their assent and I said, "They're looking for three men in them suits. We're going to be one at a time in cowboy clothes. Wilcey, you lead out first. Then Chulo and then I'll bring up the rear. Let's go. And don't none of ya'll say a goddamn word to Drake or any of his men until I get there."

After they'd got a good start, I put my horse into a little slow trot and fell into the trail. I wasn't all that surprised at how easy the robbery had gone. I'd figured it on surprise and moving quick and then that no one would fire on us, even if they got their wits about them quick enough, with Marianne in the buckboard. Of course, we still weren't home free. We had to get the money out to Drake's ranch, and then we all had to get out of that part of the country. But we were a hell of a lot closer than we'd been a few hours past.

There was a danger if someone spotted Marianne getting into Ruth's house. It'd be a little more than a coincidence, even to an idiot, that Marianne had been used by the robbers as a shield, and then here she was at the house of a lady who worked for the Cotton Exchange.

But that's why everybody don't go into the robbing business—there is an element of risk involved.

I didn't think it was too much, though. The likelihood of anyone seeing Marianne and putting two and two together was damn farfetched.

Riding along, I kept thinking about her. If the truth be told, I didn't quite know what I was going to do about her. Hell, I was about as near to being in love as you can get. But what was I going to do about it? I couldn't marry her. Or at least I didn't think I could. Why would any woman want to marry a man who was going to have to be constantly on the run and who made his living by shooting at people and getting shot at.

Yet there she was, the finest woman I'd ever known, and, with the exception of Les and Wilcey, the finest person I'd ever known. Never mind she made her living by fucking for money. Like she'd told me, "Hell, you make your living robbing and killing for money. Which is worse?"

No, Marianne wasn't no whore, not in the sense people think of a whore as.

My mind turned back to the night just before I took her to stay at Ruth's. I knew I wasn't going to be seeing her for a little while and I was about half drunk and feeling sort of mushy and kind of tender and I said to her, "You know what the two things a man most wants in a woman?"

She'd said, "No, tell me."

We were laying there in bed, holding each other, and I said, "Well, every man wants a virgin, something that no other man has ever touched. But, damn fool that a man is, he also wants her to know every trick of the trade. He wants her to be a whore at the same time." I said, "I know it ain't possible, but I want you to be my virgin whore."

Well, after a minute that set us off to laughing so hard I'd damn near thought we was going to fall out of bed, Marianne had finally said, "I don't think you can get both in the same package."

Which I'd had to agree with, laughing as hard as I was. I'd said, "Yeah, they do seem at kind of cross-purposes."

"A virgin whore!" she'd said. And started laughing again.

But then, after we'd kind of quieted down, she'd said, "That's not as funny as it seems. It's strange as hell, but sometimes, with you, I feel you're the first man I've ever known. Sometimes I feel like a virgin with you."

And I'd said, "And you damn well know everything and every way there is to please a man."

She'd turned to me. "Then maybe I am your virgin whore."

I was thinking about that as I swept through old man Drake's gate and cantered up to the ranch house. I had a kind of smile on my face.

Wilcey and Chulo and the old man were in the parlor drinking when I come clumping in, my spurs jingling against the hard floors.

First thing old man Drake asked me was, "Well? Where's the money? Ain't none of you three seem to have it."

I helped myself to the whiskey before I answered. Then I took a seat and said, "Money will be here day after tomorrow."

He said, in that old hard voice of his, "You mean you boys pulled off a job and didn't have sense enough to bring the money with you!"

I said, "No, we had better sense than to bring the money. The money will be here in two days in the company of a couple of lovely ladies. My missus being one."

He looked at me as if I was the village idiot. He said, "You ain't telling me you left a big payday in the hands of women!"

The whiskey was relaxing me. I just nodded and said, "Nothing but, old man."

He just shook his head. He said, "Well, that beats the devil to the wide. And here I thought you was a smart young man."

"Just wait and see."

We ate supper not too long after that, making do with cold beef and the other kind of poor fare that men who live by themselves make do with. The son, Amos, and two of the cowhands come in to eat with us. They didn't have much to say and neither did we, but, I tell you, that boy Amos still made me uneasy. It wasn't nothing he did or said, it was just the way he kept watching us. Twenty-five years old and still acting like a boy ain't the best situation in the world.

I asked old man Drake a little after supper if Amos and the cowhands knew what we were doing there and what we'd just done. He took a second too long to answer before he said, "They know a little. They know they ain't supposed to let on you're here. But they don't know you've done robbery." Then he flared up. He said, "But I'll damn well tell you again, that you got my word on it that ain't nobody going to give you away here. And I speak for myself and every man jack on the place!"

We went to bed not too long after that. They had some bedrooms leading off a hall that come off that main parlor, and me and Wilcey had one together. Before we settled down to sleep, he said, "Will, I'm worried about Ruth. She's all new to this business."

All I said was, "So am I."

Chapter Ten

~~~~~~

And now there wasn't anything to do but wait. I'd deemed it necessary for the girls to let a couple of days pass before they come out with the money. I'd figured that catch parties would be working alive around Houston and its environs, and, I'd figured, give it a little time, and they'd figure we was done well away and would be looking for us somewhere else. And then the girls could drive out in a buggy, like they was out for a Sunday outing, and no one would be the wiser. Of course, I'd give them the money for the good and simple reason that if any of us had been stopped on our getaway they'd of had a hell of a time proving we was the robbers without the money to back it up.

But all that good planning didn't make the waiting any easier. And it didn't keep a man from going through his head all that could go wrong.

Wilcey was well pleased with his horse. And so was I. Next morning I throwed my saddle on the bay I'd bought and took him through a little workout in the small pasture just behind the old man's house. He was all I'd figured he'd be: responsive to the rein, pretty gentle, and with that driving power under him that I knew meant quick speed and staying power. I figured, once aboard the bay any catch party was going to have a hell of a time coming up on my heel dust.

But other than seeing to the horse, doing a damn good deal of drinking, and just generally wandering around, we didn't do much else except a hell of a lot of waiting.

I had our plan for leaving the ranch and to where we were going pretty well figured out. I had decided that we were going to go to Chulo's cousin's house in San Antonio for a few days and then take the train from there and go into New Mexico and from there slip down in to old Mexico until all the hullabaloo was over with.

'Course none of it made a damn to Chulo. He was game for anything. But this time I was having to make plans for two outlaws traveling with two women, and that wasn't exactly the same thing I'd been used to.

Sunday morning come and we got up and ate breakfast. You could see the anticipation on every one of our faces. I'd taken a quick peek in that money pouch and it'd looked to be a power of money, but there was no way of telling how much.

That boy Amos was still bothering me. Right after breakfast I was standing outside staring off across the pasture, and he come out and come sidling up beside me. He said, "I hear ya'll done robbery in Houston."

I turned around and give him a quick look. He was near as tall as I was and just about as broad in the shoulders, but he still had that slack-faced expression of a boy. I said, "Didn't your daddy teach you no manners?"

But that wasn't good enough for him. He said, "I hear you been in the robbing business a good while. Is there a good deal of money in that?"

I just looked at him a long moment. Then I said, "Amos, we're here on this place by your daddy's pleasure. What you've just asked me is near about as bad as the other day when you asked to take a look at my revolver. If you ain't got no better sense than to know better, it ain't up to me to teach you." Then I turned on my heel and walked away.

Just a little before noon Wilcey come running into the house from out in the front yard. He said, "I see a buggy coming. I bet you it's them."

Well, that's what we'd been waiting for. The women and the money. I bade everyone just stay in the house and I went out on the front porch. When I got there, the buggy was just about a mile from the ranch house. I couldn't tell much about it except the dust it was throwing up. I stood out there watching it coming on, my heart in my throat.

Then, pretty soon, I got a little more worried. For as it come nearer, I could see there wasn't but one person in the buggy. Then it got near enough that I could see it was Marianne.

I was relieved, but I figured we had trouble on our hands, though I didn't exactly know what kind.

She come sweeping up in front of the ranch house, pulling the horse down to a stop, and I went out and tied him and then she come out of the buggy. The first thing she done was to fling her arms around my neck and kiss me good and hard. Then she said, "I got bad news. Ruth has run out with most of the money."

I said, "Oh, hell. I hate to tell Wilcey."

But I wasn't surprised. I'd been expecting it. I said, "Did she get it all?"

"No." She turned back to the buggy and got the pouch out. "But she took a hell of a lot of it. I've got a letter for Wilcey."

I said, "Let's just go in and do it real easy. Don't rush nothing. Watch my lead. This is damn near going to kill him."

We got on the porch and had to stop and kiss again before going in the door. She was wearing the gray dress I liked so much on her, and she just looked like the Fourth of July and Christmas all rolled in to one.

She said, smiling up into my face, "Hell, cowboy, I didn't know I could miss somebody so bad. Especially a worthless guy like you."

I just kissed her again. I didn't have anything to say to that.

We went on in the parlor. Wilcey and Chulo and the old man were sitting there. I was carrying the pouch. They got up when Marianne came in the room.

Wilcey said immediately, "Where's Ruth?"

I said, "Sit down, Wilcey. Marianne's got something to tell you."

But he wouldn't. He said, "Damnit, where's Ruth? What's happened to her?"

Marianne went over and put her hand on his chest. She said, "I've got a letter for you from her."

He jerked back, drawing himself up. "What the hell is this? What are you talking about? I want to know where the hell Ruth is!"

I said, getting close to him because I expected him to explode, I said: "She's gone, Wilcey. She's run off with most of the money. Read the letter."

He didn't explode, he just kind of sunk back down on the divan where he'd been sitting. Then he said, "What?"

I told him again.

Marianne sat down beside him. She had the letter in her hand. She said, "It's all in here, Wilcey. Read it. I'm sorry."

He took it from her and then just sat there looking at the envelope. Chulo was over by the fireplace; old man Drake, who hadn't said a word, was sitting in his straight-backed chair, staring at us all. I was just standing there looking at Wilcey.

Marianne still had the pouch. She opened it so that we could all see. She said, "It had forty-six thousand dollars in it. She took thirty thousand dollars. She left you that letter, Wilcey."

He was still turning the letter over and over in his hands. He said, "I don't believe it."

I said, "Well, I do." And I stepped forward and jerked the letter out of his hands and tore it open. I took a look at it first. It said:

> Denny
> I'm sorry but I had to leave. Please forgive me. I had burdens to pay, but I couldn't be in the kind of life you are. I took some of the money, but I left you some.

I said, "She said, she left us some of the money. *Some!*"

I turned around to Marianne. "Get us a count. Open that goddamn pouch and see how much she stole. You said she took thirty thousand out of forty-six thousand."

She looked at me, her pretty face miserable. She said, "I don't have to count it again, Will. There's sixteen thousand dollars here."

I threw the letter at Wilcey. It hit his chest and slid down to his lap. He made no effort to pick it up. I said, "There's your Ruth. Goddamn, we're robbers, but she's a thief! Just a common, garden-variety thief!"

Wilcey said, "I just can't believe this." He looked like he'd been hit in the face with an axe handle.

I turned to Marianne. "How'd it happen?"

She just shook her head. "I don't know. Ruth kept wanting to get it out and count it, even though she knew exactly how much was there. Seemed like she just liked to look at it. I thought I had it hidden from her, but she must have figured out where it was." She looked at me. "Will, I'm sorry. I guess I didn't keep a close enough eye on her."

I said, "Can't be helped."

"She must have left sometime last night, Will. I went down to the train depot and there was a north-bound train left out at four this morning. I asked about her, but nobody seemed to know. Will, I'm just really sorry."

I said, "Forget it." What I didn't say was I was just about glad it had happened. She'd eventually have done it to Wilcey, and I was glad it had happened sooner than later.

I turned to old man Drake, who was sitting there staring at me. I said, "So that's it, old man. We didn't do very well. What do we owe you?"

He said, "Well, you're the sorriest bunch of robbers I've ever seen. Trust a goddamn woman!"

I said, "Hold it. There's still a woman here and she didn't run out."

Wilcey spoke. He said, "Will, I'm leaving. I got to go look for her. I'll get the money back."

He made to get up and I put my hand in the middle of his chest and shoved him back. "No you don't. You ain't going nowhere."

One time, right after we had robbed the poker game in El Paso and we were hiding out on a rancher's place over in Mexico, a woman had run out on me. Her name had been Linda, the same as the little highborn senorita's, but there the comparison had ended. She was nothing but straight tramp. I just didn't know it at the time. When word had come to me, through the rancher, that she'd sold me out to a cheap Mexican politico, I'd been fixing to go back to town and look for her. And that with every lawman on both sides of the border looking for me. When it happened, Chulo and Wilcey and the rancher had knocked me out and tied me to a chair until I could come to my senses.

I stood over Wilcey and reminded him of the occasion.

He said, "It's different, Will. I got to go."

I said, "It ain't a damn bit different."

He said, "Yes it is. She was a bad woman. Ruth ain't. I got to find her and straighten her out." He said it with a face that looked like a pile of dead ashes in a long since used campfire.

I leaned toward him. "Wilcey, she's gone. She ain't ever going to change. She was bad news from the first. I knew this was going to happen. Now let it be."

He said, "I can't."

God, the sucker looked miserable. I knew how he felt, but there wasn't a damn thing I could do for him. He tried to get up again and I pushed him back down. "Don't, Will," he said. "I got to go."

I said, "Listen, every lawman in this county is looking for somebody that looks just like you. What are you going to do? Go down to the train station and ask questions? They'd have you in jail in five minutes."

He wouldn't listen. He put on his hat and said, "Will, I got to go. I got to find her."

I stepped back and pointed at Chulo. "Com'ere, Nigger." Chulo got up. I said, "He don't get off that goddamn divan. You understand?"

He said, "*Si. Yo comprendo.*" And he didn't smile when he said it.

Hell, I could feel for Wilcey. After his wife had run out on him, he'd been the most cynical man about women I'd ever seen. And here another one had done it to him. But I was his friend and I wasn't

going to see him get his ass killed because of Ruth. So
I was doing what I had to do.

I guess then was the finest thing I'd ever seen a
woman do. At that second Marianne moved down the
divan and put her arms around Wilcey and said, "I
know it hurts. But right now don't think about it."

He started crying. That was how bad he was hurting. I guess it was the first time I'd ever seen a grown
man cry, and it embarrassed us all. To hide my face I
turned to old man Drake and said, "All right, all we
got was what you've heard. What do we owe you?"

Well, he looked at me. But he didn't look at me
with those old hard eyes. Instead he kind of stroked
that old scraggly mustache and said, "Looks like you
boys have been running in hard luck. Don't seem like
you've made a very good payday for the work you've
been through. Why don't you just leave me a
hundred dollars to make up for all the whiskey
you've drank."

Well, I was that surprised. If you'd asked me if the
old man was anyone who gave a shit what happened
to his fellow citizen, I'd of damn near died laughing.
And here he was asking for only a hundred dollars.

I started to say something and Wilcey said, "Will,
tell Chulo to get out from in front of me. I know he
does your bidding and I don't want to kill him."

I wheeled on him. I pointed my finger, fixing to say
something.

In that instant Amos and two of the ranchhands
come through the door. They were all carrying rifles
and they had them pointed at us.

I stopped what I was fixing to say and just stared at
them. It was the damnedest turn of events I'd ever ex-
perienced. I said, "What the hell!"

Amos was to my left of the three of them. He said,
"Well, Mister Smart Aleck Robber, the laugh's on
you. We'll just take that money." And he cocked the

goddamn hammer of the Winchester he was holding. "Now hand it over. And maybe we won't bury you behind the barn."

Old man Drake was sitting in his chair just to my left. Chulo was kind of to my right, in front of the couch. Wilcey was still seated. Marianne had pulled slightly back from him. Amos and the two ranch-hands were standing right in front of us, their backs to the wall. I turned to the old man. I was mad as hell. I said, "Is this the way you keep your word?"

The old man was looking at his son in what I considered amazement. He didn't even look around at me. He just said, "Boy, you put that rifle down and get the hell out of here!"

Amos said, looking at me, "No, papa. They got money and we going to get it. Now you just set down there and shush up."

The old man, just kind of drawing himself up like a banty cock, stood up and started walking toward the boy. He said, "Goddamnit, don't you understand that these are guests in our home and you don't disgrace this place! Now you give me that rifle!"

He got in front of Amos, and in that instant I drew and Chulo drew. I shot the man in the middle, the slug taking him square in the middle of the chest, driving him back up against the wall, and Chulo shot the one to our right. I just caught a glimpse of that because I was already wheeling around on Amos. He'd been hidden to my view by his daddy being in front of him, but then the rifle in his hand went off and his daddy fell backward and then the rifle boomed twice again as I went down on one knee, my arm extended, snapshooting that revolver of mine. I got him just under the throat and shot him twice more as he went down. But he went down with slugs tearing out of that Winchester.

All of a sudden it was very quiet. Unless you've

heard it, you can't imagine how loud the reports from high-caliber small arms can sound in a small room. I couldn't remember distinctly, but it seemed as if the two ranchhands had got off a shot apiece before Chulo and I had killed them.

I got up slowly from the knee I'd been down on. The room was filled with blue smoke from the explosions of the cartridges that had been fired.

The old man was down on his back. The three we'd killed were slumped against the wall. I walked over to him, holstering my revolver as I did. The old man had his hands clawed in front of his chest as if he'd been trying to ward off the fatal blow his son had dealt him. I looked down at him. He was dead all right. I said, "Well, this is a hell of a mess."

Then behind me I heard Wilcey say, "Will. You better come quick."

I turned. Marianne was still sitting on the couch, but she was doubled over. I went to her side, raising her face. I said, "What's the matter, darling?"

She just give me a grimace for an answer.

Then I looked to where her hands were pressing against her sides. Blood was running out between her fingers.

I said, "Oh, shit!"

And my heart went hollow inside me. I very carefully took her under the chin and got her to sit back on the divan. Then, when she was leaned back, I took her hands away from where she had them pressed.

I've tended to a lot of my partners that was shot. It is something else to tend to the women you love.

She had been sitting sideways to the gunfire, and the bullet, from what little I could tell, had come quartering across her, striking her in the rib cage about midway and then going on out the other side. As delicately as I could I felt the two wounds. It had broke the rib, sure enough, but as near as I could tell, it hadn't nicked the lung. At least there was none of that pink froth coming out that tells you you got a lung-shot customer.

My heart was nearly stopping. I said to Wilcey, "Find some rags and boil them in water. Chulo, you get out of here. I got to take her bodice down."

Which was kind of a funny thing to say. Here she was, hurt, and I was worrying about another man seeing her. And she'd been a whore and no telling how many men had seen her. But that was the way I was feeling, no matter how unreasonable it was.

I unbuttoned her bodice. Fortunately it went all the way down to her waist. Then I kind of eased her forward so I could slip it off over her shoulders and get her arms out. I said, "Does it hurt real bad, honey?"

She shook her head no, but she had her lips pressed together so that I knew she was lying.

After that I took out my knife and cut through her underclothes, the slips and petticoats and what not.

It nearly made me cry, seeing those ugly wounds against her smooth, creamy skin. The wound going in wasn't so bad, but it had come out leaving a gaping, ugly hole. I said, "Oh, shit!"

Then I looked up at her. She had her eyes open, watching me. I said, "It ain't real bad, honey. Course ain't no gunshot good, but it didn't hit anything vital. I think it might have broken a rib, judging from some little bone splinters I can see. The main thing to worry about is infection. I've had considerable experience treating these matters, and you're going to be all right." She looked like she was getting mighty pale. I said, "Don't pass out, honey, for God's sake."

She nodded real quick and then shut her eyes. She had her hands down by her side, her fists clenched tightly.

About then Wilcey yelled in from the kitchen. He said, "This water's boiling. How long you want me to boil these rags?"

"About five minutes," I yelled. "But when you take them up don't touch them with your hands. Use the point of your knife."

I got Marianne to kind of turn around on the divan and lay back. I put my hand on her face and smoothed her skin. She opened her eyes and half smiled at me. She said, "I never been shot before."

I said, "Hell, ain't nothing to it. I been shot a half dozen times, and it ain't no more bother than a head cold. Sometimes it kept me from going to Sunday school when I meant to, but other than that it was no bother."

She kind of chuckled a little. Then she said, "Damn, don't make me laugh. It don't feel real good."

I looked at her, feeling very sorry for the condition I'd got her in. But I knew I couldn't have foreseen it. There was no way I was going to figure that boy Amos was going to come in and try to stick up three hardcase robbers.

Wilcey came in, carrying the rags on the point of his knife. He glanced down at Marianne's bare bosom and then looked quickly away. I took the haft of the knife from him, waving the rags around in the air so they'd cool. I said, "Where's Chulo?"

"He's out in front, I think. Watching."

I said, "Hand me that bottle of whiskey and then you go out and help him."

He left and I set the bottle down beside me and felt the rags to see if they were cool enough to put on her bare skin. They were and I laid them on her middle for the moment. Then I picked up the bottle of whiskey. I said to her, "Honey, this is going to hurt like hell, but there's no help for it. I got to pour this whiskey on there. It keeps it from getting infected."

I turned her over on her side a little so the whiskey would run into the wound. I tell you, my hands were just all sweaty. I'd doctored plenty of gunshot partners, but this was different.

She must have felt it for she said, "Go ahead. Get it over with."

Well, I doused it damn good with that whiskey. She didn't scream, but she done everything else. She jerked and trembled and gritted her teeth until it was hurting me damn near more than I could stand.

Finally, I finished. I said, "That's near about it."

She kind of gasped. "Thank God!"

"But I got to poke these rags in each end of the wound. See, if I don't do that it'll heal over from the outside, and we need it to heal from the inside out. That way we won't get no infection."

I said, "Now I got to poke these rags in the holes. And it'll hurt, but it won't be as bad."

With trembling fingers I took the rags and shoved one in each hole. She flinched, but I could tell it hadn't been as bad. After that I turned her over again on her back. She was pale and sweating.

I said, "I'm sorry, baby." I kind of pulled her underclothes back together, covering up her breasts. I said, "I'll be right back."

I went in the bedroom I'd been sleeping in and got the blanket I'd used and took it back and covered her up with it. She still had her face held tight against the pain. I stroked her soft skin and said, "I feel like hell about this, Marianne. Last thing I wanted was for you to get hurt knowing me. I should have never got you in on this."

She said, her voice a little weak, "You didn't get me involved, cowboy. I got myself in on this. And I still ain't sorry."

I got up. "Let me get Chulo and Wilcey back in here. We got to figure out something in a hurry."

I went to the door and called them in. Standing a little way away from the divan, I told them what I had in mind. "Listen, this place is fixing to get hotter than a burning barn. Wilcey, you and Chulo go ahead and saddle up and take off. I guess you'd be safer in San Antonio than anyplace else I can think of."

Wilcey said, "What are you going to do, Will?"

I hesitated. My head was whirling with so much worry about Marianne that I couldn't think. I said, "We're going to stay here a little while and then I'm going to take her to a doctor in Houston."

Wilcey said, "I thought you said it didn't hit none of her vitals?"

"It didn't. But it might have broken a rib."

He said, "Will, do you think she's going to die from that wound? Do you think it's that serious?"

I shook my head. "No, I don't think so. It didn't hit nothing except meat and bone."

"Well, you take her to a doctor in Houston and they're going to put you in jail. That is, if they don't find you here first. You ain't forgot you told me there was the boy and three other hands." He gestured at the bodies against the wall. "That's just the son and two of them. That other'n may be on the outside of the range, but he could show back up here anytime."

I just shook my head. "That's a chance I got to take."

He said, "But they'll put Marianne in jail too. It won't be hard for them to connect her up to this robbery. You might get her to a doctor, but you'll also get her in jail."

Just then she called me from the couch. I went over. "What is it, honey?"

She said, "You're not going to take me to a doctor in Houston. And I don't want to argue about it."

Wilcey came over. He put his hand on my shoulder. "Will, you better let me do the thinking right now. You ain't doing too good of a job of it."

I stood there, trying to decide. It was true that her wound wasn't that dangerous, and it was also true that sure as I took her to a doctor in Houston we'd both be in jail. I looked down at her. I said, "We ought to go to San Antonio. There's doctors there that would be safe. But it's a long, rough trip for you. All I could do would be to put you in the seat of that buggy and it'll take us two or three days. Can you take it?"

She nodded. "Of course. That's the only thing to do. Will you be safe in San Antonio?"

I shrugged. "Safer than most places."

"Then let's do that."

I turned to Wilcey and Chulo. "Ya'll go ahead and start for San Antonio. I'll follow with Marianne as soon as I can. We'll meet at Chulo's cousin's house if we make it."

But Wilcey shook his head. "No, Will. We'll all go together. You and her in that buggy would be sitting ducks."

"They're looking for three men, Wilcey. Ain't no use you and Chulo buying into this trouble."

He said, "Yeah, they is a use. We're partners. You ain't going to be able to outrun nobody in that buggy, and if it comes to a fight, three guns are going to be a hell of a lot better than one. And ain't no use arguing about it. I figured on this from you, and Chulo and I done talked it over. We're sticking."

I looked down at my boots for a minute and then over at Marianne. Finally, I said, "All right. And I appreciate it. Maybe if I didn't think it was best for Marianne I wouldn't let you do it, but she makes it all different." Then I said, "Chulo, you go and get the horses up and get them saddled. Will, you rummage around in that kitchen and find all the grub you can. I'll get Marianne ready and get her in the buggy."

Chapter Eleven

~~~~~~

We got away about an hour later, Wilcey and Chulo ranged out beside the buggy as outriders and my horse tied on behind. We'd made Marianne as comfortable as we could with all the blankets we could find in the house, but it was still going to be a rough ride. I was going cross country, avoiding the roads, and every time the buggy bumped you could see how it hurt her.

We traveled on and on that first evening, trying to put as much distance between us and Houston as we could. By luck we hadn't seen anyone, but that didn't mean they weren't around.

We kept on that night until I judged it was near nine or ten o'clock. I had hated to travel in the dark, for I couldn't see the rough places very well and I knew the rough traveling was a hardship on Marianne.

But she never said a word. After I'd doctored the wounds I'd wrapped some long rags tightly around her midriff to try and keep the bleeding down. And once she'd complained it was a little too tight so I'd stopped and loosed them. Other than that she hadn't had much to say.

We finally made a camp in a little grove of trees. I debated about building a fire, but decided against it.

I calculated we'd made twenty miles from Houston and I figured that was still too close. Wilcey had found some cold beef and biscuits and we made out on that. I'd of liked to have fixed Marianne some broth, but we'd of needed a fire for that and the risk wasn't worth it. Still, she did get a little of the beef down, though it took a considerable amount of urging to get her to do it. I knew the feeling after you've been shot, but you've got to force yourself to eat to keep your strength up.

I sat by her in the buggy until her breathing became kind of even and I figured she was asleep, and then I wandered over and sat down by Wilcey and Chulo.

They had their backs up against a couple of trees and were smoking and drinking whiskey. Wilcey handed me the bottle and I had a pull. Then I lit a cigarillo. He said, "How's she doing?"

"Pretty good, considering. Little pretty women don't handle gunshot wounds as good as men. But she ain't running no fever yet. I felt of her just before I come over and she felt pretty cool."

He said thoughfully, "She's a damn good woman, Will."

All I could see of him in the dark was the glow of his cigarillo. He said, "I was pretty wrong about her. Her and Ruth. Wasn't I?"

I just said, "I'm sorry for your trouble, Wilcey. I know how you must be feeling right now."

He said, "It don't matter." Then he flipped his cigarillo away in the dark; it made a low arc and then hit, landing with a sputter of sparks.

I knew it did matter. But I didn't say anything. I knew he was hurting like hell, but there ain't much a man can say to a friend at such a time.

After a minute he said, "I don't see how I could have been so damn wrong. I just don't understand.

And how come you could see her the way she really was? You, who didn't know her. And me, being in her bed, eating with her, talking with her. And I didn't see it. I must be seven kinds of a fool."

I said, "Wilcey, just figure it's going to eat on you for a long time. And it'll hurt. But you'll get over it."

"Goddamnit!" he said. He got out a cigarillo and lit it with a lucifer. In the glow of the match I could see the misery in his face. He said, "Well, we found out who the real whore was, didn't we. And it wasn't Marianne."

I said, "Wilcey, let it alone. That's all you can do. Just figure you're like me—you just never had no luck with women."

He said: "Seems like you're doing all right now."

I just said, "Maybe."

Which was true. After she got well, where were we going and what were we going to do? What the hell kind of life could I offer her? A life of fear and running? A life of gunshot wounds? A life of being hunted?

Hell, she was a sweet, soft woman. She wouldn't be able to take much of that.

After a while I got up and went back to the buggy. Marianne was still sleeping. I lay down on the floor of the buggy right below her. I wanted to be close in case she got to feeling bad.

By mid-afternoon next day Marianne was running a fever. I opened her dress and took the bandages off. The wound looked a little red, but it wasn't all that bad. But she was mighty hot.

I said, "We got to make some tracks. I got to get her to a doctor in San Antonio."

We took to the road that second day, and I made that buggy horse step. We camped late that night and she was hot as ever and a little light-headed.

I said, "Baby, I'm worried about you, but I'm doing all I can."

She put her hand up and stroked my forehead. "Don't worry. It'll be all right. I got you and that's all that matters."

She was sicker the next day. I looked at the wound again, and though it was a little redder, it wasn't bad enough to be causing such a fever. But, hell, I didn't know nothing about a female with a gunshot wound.

When we camped that night, I knew it was going to be bad. And it was. She was plenty sick and getting more and more light-headed all the time. I couldn't get any food down her, and that was worrying the hell out of me. Chulo and Wilcey knew how I was feeling, and they were mighty kind about giving me all the help they could. But there wasn't any help for it.

I left her for a few minutes to sit around the fire with them. Wilcey said, "Will, I'm sorry as hell about the money. I know how risky that robbery was, and we ought to of made a better payday if it hadn't of been for Ruth. I want you to keep my share of what little she didn't steal."

I could just see his face in the small glow of the campfire. I said, with some disgust, "Well, I see your brains are still addled. Do you think I give a goddamn about that money? You take my share. How's that?"

He just looked away. I knew how bad he felt. Hell, I was near worried sick myself.

We got in to San Antonio about noon of the next day and headed directly for Chulo's cousin's house. Chulo's cousin was a big dealer in the stolen cattle that were driven up from Mexico. He was a good little fat man, and he and his wife bustled around and got Marianne to bed in one of their small, cool rooms. I sent Chulo immediately to bring back a doctor.

I said, "Just bring one. Whether he wants to come or not."

Then I sat by Marianne's bed and held her hand while I waited. She was mighty hot and mighty out of her head. Wilcey brought me in a bottle of whiskey and a pitcher of water and a glass. Then he left.

It was a long time before the doctor came, and I had a lot of time to think, except I didn't want to think. I didn't want to think what would happen if Marianne didn't make it. She'd become mighty important to me in the short time I'd known her.

When the doctor finally showed up, I wasn't too pleased. He had the smell of whiskey on his breath and he looked a little seedy. He didn't pay much attention to me, but set at his work. Chulo's cousin's wife brought in a good lamp, and by that light he undressed Marianne from the nightgown Chulo's cousin's wife had got her in and made an examination.

All he did was grunt and say, "Uh huh."

Finally, I said, "Well?"

He said, "She's mighty sick. I got to get these bone splinters out. You better turn your head because it ain't going to be pretty."

I said, "I can stand it."

"Send for some help," he said, "to hold her down."

Wilcey and Chulo came into the room, and Chulo took her by the shoulders and pressed them down against the bed. Wilcey stood beside me, with his hand on my arm. I was grateful for that, for it was harder to stand than I'd thought. As the doctor probed and she'd jerk, even though she was half unconscious, my heart would nearly stop.

When he was finally through, I was bathed in sweat. He bandaged her back up with proper cloth, snapped his little bag shut, and said, "I'll be back to-morrow. Keep her well covered. You got to try and sweat that fever out of her. If she comes to, try and get as much whiskey down her as you can. I've done all I can. She's a mighty sick lady."

He left. Chulo came to stand in front of me. He just looked down. I said, "Thanks, *amigo*."

He didn't smile. I'd never seen the Nigger look so troubled. He said, "No *importa, mi amigo*. What you want Chulo to do?"

"Nothing," I said. "Just what you been doing."

He said, "I can't keel the mens who shot her again. I would if I could."

I said, "I know."

He left and then Wilcey said, "Will, I'm going to bring you in some food. I know for a fact you ain't eat or slept much these last few days."

I said, "No, I ain't hungry."

He stood a minute more. "I don't know what to say."

"Neither do I," I said.

He said, "I'm sorry about this."

"Never mind, Wilcey. You're still my partner. You've been a good friend through this, even though I know you've had troubles of your own."

He touched me on the shoulder and left.

I sat there, the lamp up bright, holding Marianne's hand. I had her well bundled up with blankets. I just sat there thinking, trying to figure out in my mind what was worth what. We'd pulled a robbery that had netted each of us more than the average man made in a year. But still we'd been cheated in the process. And we'd caused the deaths of four men. Was it worth it? Hell, I didn't know. I didn't know nothing except I was a robber and loved the woman that was laying on the bed.

Because if she didn't make it, I wasn't going to

make it so good myself. I didn't know where our future was going, but I knew mine wouldn't be worth a damn without her.

I sat there through the long hours of the night. I was dead tired, but I couldn't have laid down and slept if my life had depended on it. All I could do was sit there by her bedside and watch her face in the glow of the lantern.

Just before dawn her eyes flickered open. She looked over at me, puzzled. I reached over and felt her forehead. It was cool. Her fever had broke.

I said, "Howdy."

She looked at me a long moment, and then a little half smile come on her face. She said, "Where the hell are we?"

I said, "Oh, taking a little vacation."

I was so goddamn relieved I couldn't even see straight. I reached over and poured her out a glass of whiskey and leaned over and held it to her lips. I said, "How about a drink? Doctor's orders."

She looked at me and said, "Hell, ever since I've known you I've had nothing but trouble."

I said, "I know. I feel the same about you. But I'm worth it. Now drink the goddamn whiskey."

We were going to be all right.

DELL'S ACTION-PACKED WESTERNS

Selected Titles

Dell Bestsellers